Trainwreck

Soulless Kings MC

Andi Rhodes

Blue Journey Publishing

Copyright © 2022 by Andi Rhodes

All rights reserved.

No part of this book may be reproduced in any form or by any electronic or mechanical means, including information storage and retrieval systems, without written permission from the author, except for the use of brief quotations in a book review.

Cover Artwork - © Amanda Walker PA & Design Services

Also by Andi Rhodes

Broken Rebel Brotherhood

Broken Souls

Broken Innocence

Broken Boundaries

Broken Rebel Brotherhood: Complete Series Box set

Broken Rebel Brotherhood: Next Generation

Broken Hearts

Broken Wings

Broken Mind

Bastards and Badges

Stark Revenge

Slade's Fall

Jett's Guard

Soulless Kings MC

Fender

Joker

Piston

Greaser

Riker

Trainwreck

Squirrel

Gibson

Satan's Legacy MC

Snow's Angel

Toga's Demons

Magic's Torment

A note from the author:

Trainwreck is the sixth book in my Soulless Kings MC series and while it can be read as a standalone, it will definitely be more enjoyable if read in order. There is a major story arc that carries over from several of the series' books. Also, please note that this book does end on a cliffhanger... sort of. The main characters get their HEA, as all of my characters do; however, book seven is set up in Trainwreck. That being said, you DO NOT have to read Trainwreck to read and enjoy the next book because there will be a bit of recap.

Now that all my warnings are out of the way, I hope you enjoy Trainwreck and Sylvia's story!

Much love,
Andi

Prologue

When shit spins out of control, robs more years of your life, takes over your every waking moment... that's when you realize that planning is pointless and decimating the evil in the world takes away your soul.

Trainwreck
Two years earlier...

I've spent the last twelve years being kicked in the balls with one disappointment after another. Fuck, my twin sister was declared dead. Kidnapped, missing, dead. That's a blow no little kid should have to feel, yet here I am, older, possibly wiser, and still waiting for another kick to the balls.

I sit in my chair in the meeting room, the one where the Soulless Kings' hold church, and watch the woman claiming to be my dead sister, Trinity, pace.

"Would you sit the fuck down?"

She glares at me and unceremoniously plops into a chair at the other end of the table and huffs out a breath. Instead of huffing, she should be thanking whatever the fuck she believes in that she's even here because if this were church instead of a 'casual' meeting, she'd be relegated to anywhere else but this room.

A cell phone rings, cutting through the tension in the space. Riker lifts his cell off the table and smiles after looking at the screen.

"David, give me some good news," he says when he presses it against his ear.

David is his contact who was willing to run the woman's DNA to determine who the fuck she is. We all watch as his smile falls, and he mumbles 'uh huh' several times and nods. "Well, thanks for the info." Riker rolls his eyes. "Yeah, fine, I'll find time, and I'll be there."

"What's the verdict?" Greaser asks, impatience in his tone.

"The Nightmare Room is going to have a guest soon," Riker deadpans.

Unable to control my reaction, I shoot up from his chair and lunge across the table at the imposter. Everything seems to happen in slow motion. Fender jumps up and reaches for my ankle while Joker latches onto my leg. Greaser manages to grab ahold of my arm a moment before I make contact with her.

"Let me go," I seethe, straining against the men holding me.

"Not gonna happen," Fender barks. "Either get your emotions in check or you're outta here."

"But you heard him, Prez!" I yell. "Riker said she's headed for—"

"Not what I said, bro," Riker states. All eyes turn to him for clarification. "The Nightmare Room will be used for David."

"What?" Greaser asks. "Fuck, just tell us what the hell he said."

"Trinity's DNA is a match for the sample from the hairbrush Trainwreck gave us to compare to."

Trinity's shoulders slump, almost as if she's relieved to finally be validated, and she bores her eyes into mine. I can't look away. I try but fail miserably. The fight in me drains from my body, and my eyes well up.

"Trinity?" I question. "Trin?"

She doesn't say a word. For a moment, anger weaves through me again, but it's gone just as quickly. Trinity's in shock, just like me, and it might take a while to get used to this whole 'risen from the dead' thing.

"Jesus," Fender mumbles as he releases me. "I don't know what to say."

"If David confirmed Trinity's identity, what did he do wrong?" Greaser asks.

Rather than answer, Riker shifts his attention to Trinity. "Who's Sarah Lowell?"

Trinity's face pales, and when she flattens her palms on the table and stands, she sways on her feet almost to the point where I worry she's going to pass out. None of the other men in the room seem concerned... well, none except Greaser. Despite his resistance to her, I can see something in his eyes whenever she's near, and right now is no different.

And the next few moments are proof of exactly that.

"Trinity?" Greaser rushes to her side and wraps an arm around her waist to hold her up. "Who is she?"

Time stands still as she starts to collapse. Greaser maintains his hold on her as she goes down.

"Trin!" he yells. "Trinity!"

He finally lifts her in his arms, just as she's about to hit the floor. What the fuck he was waiting for, I'll never know, but I'll also never forget the way my feet refused to budge so I could be the one to save her, the one to do what I couldn't all those years ago.

"Hey, there you are," Greaser says, his tone gritty.

Someone clears their throat behind Greaser, and he turns, with Trinity in his arms, and I see Fender and the others staring expectantly for her to answer Riker's question.

"I... Sarah..." A tremble rolls through Trinity's body. "Sarah is me. I am Sarah."

"What?" Greaser snaps and practically drops her to her feet. "What the fuck does that mean?"

The glue seems to disappear as my feet carry me to Greaser and Trinity's side.

"I don't understand," I say, shaking my head. "The DNA confirms you're Trinity."

"Riker," Fender begins. "Tell us exactly what David said."

"He said what I told you, that her DNA..." He nods at Trinity. "It matches what he tested it against on the hairbrush. But apparently, he felt the need to take it a step further."

"Just fucking spit it out, bro," Greaser demands.

"He also ran Trinity's fingerprints into some system he developed for Inroad Technologies and came back with a match to a missing person named Sarah Lowell."

"How the hell did he get my fingerprints?"

"Apparently, he was able to pull them from the tube he had you place the swab in."

"Did you ask him to run fingerprints?" Fender asks.

"Fuck no, I didn't," Riker snaps and turns to Greaser. "You were there. I never once mentioned fingerprints."

"I know," Greaser confirms. "Did he say why he ran them?"

Riker heaves a sigh. "He said he thought he was doing me a solid by trying to gather as much info as possible."

"Some favor," Trinity mumbles.

"Trin, why would your fingerprints match someone else?" I ask, clearly confused.

"Because that's who I was for the last twelve years." She sits in a chair and drops her head into her hands. "I..." She shifts her gaze, taking in each man in the room. "I wasn't trying to lie to you. You have to believe me. I just... After I was taken, Ma and Pa changed my identity. In less than twenty-four hours, I became Sarah Lowell. I became their daughter."

"That doesn't make sense. If they kidnapped you, why on Earth would they have your fingerprints done and entered into a system?"

I stare at Trinity as she seems to come up with an answer that will make sense to all of us.

"Because to them, I was their daughter. They did everything they could to make sure we appeared as normal a family as possible. Including submitting my fingerprints for some program that was supposed to help ensure child safety."

"And you let them?"

The accusatory quality in my question sparks Trinity's temper.

"I was nine!" she shouts. "They told me that mom and dad didn't want me anymore. They made me believe they were all I had. What was I supposed to do?"

My face hardens, the muscles seemingly fused into a permanent state of fury. "I'll fucking kill 'em."

"Yeah, probably," Fender agrees. "But first, we need to

figure out what the hell we do now. If David entered her fingerprints into a system, she can be tracked. We don't want that."

Trinity snaps her gaze to Fender. "Wait, you think they can track me here?"

"I don't know," Fender answers honestly. "Are they good with technology? Do they have the means to track you, the connections?"

"I... probably." My gut twists when her eyes fill with tears. "They managed to make the world believe I was dead. They were able to give me a new identity that no one questioned for twelve years." A tear slides down her cheek, and even as she swipes at it, I realize I want to make them go away for her. "Yeah, I think they have connections."

"That's not gonna happen." I snap out the vow as I kneel next to Trinity's chair and rest a hand on her arm. "They won't find you here. They won't take you again."

"No fucking way," Greaser agrees.

"Prez, we need a plan... fast." Joker sits down in the chair he occupied earlier. "We need every single voting member in here because I have a feeling things are about to get ugly."

"He's right," Piston says as he also sits.

Fender pulls his cell phone out of his pocket, and his fingers fly over the screen. When he sets the device down, he sits at the head of the table.

"Church starts in ten," he says. "Trainwreck, why don't you take Trinity to one of the rooms and we'll—"

"I'm not leaving," I bark. "No disrespect, Prez, but she's my sister. I want to be involved in this every step of the way."

Fender stares at me for a moment before nodding. "Fine." He shifts his focus to Trinity. "Trinity, you can't be in here during church. Why don't you go out to the main room and wait for us to finish?"

Trinity shakes her head wildly as she fidgets with her hands. "I can't... what if... I don't—"

"I'll stay with her," Greaser says. "I vote in favor of finding, torturing, and killing these motherfuckers. As long as that's the plan..." He bangs a fist on the table two times.

Fender locks eyes with Greaser for a moment, questions dancing in his eyes, questions he doesn't ask. "Noted. I'll allow your vote. Now get her outta here."

Greaser grips Trinity's bicep and urges her to stand. He guides her toward the door, but I stop them in their tracks.

"Don't let her out of your sight," I command, and they both look over their shoulders at me. I lower my chin before speaking again. "I did that once." I lift my head and lock eyes with Greaser. "Just... don't take your eyes off of her."

"I won't."

Those two words from Greaser are controlled and full of promise. Why then, do I feel like shit's about to hit the fan, no matter how much planning or plotting the Soulless Kings' do?

"I promise you, Trainwreck. I've got her."

In this moment, I soak up the words and make an honest effort to believe them. I give him a curt nod, and he and my sister disappear from the room.

Sometimes putting your faith in someone is the hardest thing to do, and there's a reason for that. Not everything goes the way you hope. And when shit spins out of control, robs more years of your life, takes over your every waking moment... that's when you realize that planning is pointless and decimating the evil in the world takes away your soul.

Chapter One

You must not have asked the right questions then. Because if you had, you'd know that I can't be won over with sweet talk.

Sylvia

Present day...

"I'm going to hang up now."

I roll my eyes at my sister, Charlie, grateful she can't see me because if she could, I'd probably get slapped across the face... with love, of course.

"We haven't talked in weeks," I remind her. "Why should we wait another day?"

"Syl, it won't even be a full twenty-four hours," Charlie says on a sigh. "I can barely hear you with the blaring music in the background." She pauses. "What is that song? I recognize..."

The rest of her words trail off as strong arms wrap around my waist from behind. I glance over my shoulder and see Brick standing there, head bent to kiss my neck.

"Oh, hey, Charlie," I say in between shaky breaths. "I gotta go."

Brick shoves his hand inside my jeans, and then my panties, and starts rubbing my clit. I grind against his palm, my body begging for more. I don't worry about the party raging around us. Black Savages know how to be loud and obnoxious, and quite frankly, there's not a girl in this place who wouldn't wish she were me right now.

"Seriously?" Charlie sounds angry, but I have no idea why. "You just told me how we couldn't wait one more day to talk and now you're bailing? What the fuck Syl?"

Oh, that.

"Sorry," I mumble, my brain not firing on all cylinders with the magic Brick is creating between my thighs. "Love y—"

Brink ends the call. I tilt my head back to look at him and frown. "That was fucking rude. I was about to hang up. I didn't need you to do it for me."

Brick removes his hand and glares at me. "If you'd rather gossip on the phone than find someplace private to ride my cock, here you go." He thrusts my cell phone at me. "I'm not gonna do this dance tonight."

With that, he turns and walks away. I hang my head as I pull in a deep breath and hold it until my head starts to spin. Anger at Brick infuses every cell in my body, and I lift my head to glare at his retreating back. He's good at this... at making me feel like I'm the only girl in the room, and then, just as quickly, making me feel like I did something wrong when he's clearly the asshole.

I lift my phone and glance at the screen before letting out a groan. To call or not to call... that is the question. Memories of how I was treated growing up, always in second place, always the younger one, the unimportant one, flood my brain.

Fuck it!

I'm not in the mood for the vicious cycle that phone call would lead to. I'll apologize for the hang-up, she won't accept it. And then the cycle will start. Charlie will lecture me on all the ways I'm failing in life, which then leads to the whole 'you're better than this' speech.

Don't get me wrong, I love my sister, but since she married Fender, I'm actually someone who exists to my family. The Black Savages take me seriously now. They see me. And I have no intention of changing that.

I shove my phone into my back pocket, grinning at the way my jeans hug my curves. Screw Brick. I don't need him to have a good time. I cross the room and get another beer. Leaning back against the bar, my foot propped on the railing at the bottom, I scan the room for someone to help me turn the night around.

Finally, my eyes land on a man I've never seen before. He's wearing jeans, boots, a white T-shirt and black leather jacket. Nothing about him indicates he's part of a club, which is fine with me. I don't want the hassle of explaining why I'm fucking a potential enemy, nor do I want to feel like I have to be on guard while all I want is a man to finish what Brick started.

"He's trouble."

I whip my head to the right and see Donovan standing there. Ever since he took over as president of Black Savages MC, he's made it his duty to not only protect the club, but to also protect the women within the club, whether we want it or not. In case you're wondering, I most definitely *do not*.

But I get it. Once it was discovered what Leal, our former president and someone who Charlie and I looked up to as an uncle, had done to Charlie, everyone was a bit on edge. If our president could do those things to a little girl he supposedly loved so much, what else had he done, what else was he capable of?

"What are you talking about?" I ask, a bite in my tone.

Donovan nods toward the man who caught my eye. "Pete. He's trouble. Find someone else."

"How do you know he's trouble?" I ask, needing to know, unable to accept what anyone says as truth unless they have evidence to back it up. "He's here, so I can't imagine he's done anything too terrible."

Donovan shakes his head at me. "Sylvia, why can't you ever just accept what I tell you? He's trouble. That's all you need to know, and the fact that I'm the Black Savages' president should be enough for you—"

"For me to what?" I arch a brow. "Believe every word that comes out of your mouth?" I scoff. "Yeah, that would be smart. Or are you forgetting how many times I believed Leal, how many times *you* believed him, no questions asked?"

Donovan heaves a sigh and takes one last hit of his cigarette. He twists toward the bar top, drops it into a glass with some melted ice, and it hisses as the cherry is put out.

"I'm not going to argue with you, Syl," he says, sounding all kinds of resigned. "But as much as I'm not a fan of whatever game you and Brick are playing with each other, I'm even less okay with the idea of you and Pete." Donovan rests his hand on my shoulder. "You're a grown ass woman and you can do what you want, yes, but I will always be around to nudge you in the right direction. You're not the only one who carries scars from the time Leal was president. I do too. We all were fooled. So I'm trying to do things differently."

"But telling me what to do isn't different, Donovan," I

huff out. "Leal controlled every aspect of all of our lives, whether we knew it or not." I narrow my eyes at him. "Don't do that. Don't be that kind of president. Because we're not *only* Black Savages or the family of a Black Savage. We're people, with lives outside of this place, with dreams and needs that don't always mean staying here to play the good little soldier. Besides, I'm not a member. I'm just a girl whose father was president many years ago."

Donovan brushes a strand of hair behind my ear. "You're more than that, Sylvia, and you know it."

The gesture, and the vehement way he says the words, don't do anything for me. Someone looking on might think we're lovers, but we never have been. Donovan is a great guy, and I love him, but not like that. He's family, end of story.

I push off the bar and take a step away before turning to face him. "Jesus, when did you become so sappy?" I joke.

"Whatever," he returns. He gets just as uncomfortable as I do in these kinds of situations. But we still subject ourselves to them. "Just be careful, okay? And if you're intent on Pete, I'll back off. But I'm still just a phone call away... always."

"I know." I lean forward and kiss him on the cheek, much like I would a big brother. "And you don't have to worry about me. I'll be fine."

I toss my hair over my shoulder and pivot to face the crowd. I hear Donovan mumbling something under his breath, but I can't make out the words. No doubt he's asking whatever the fuck he believes in to give him strength to deal with me. It's kinda his thing.

I weave through the bodies, never stopping to chit-chat with anyone, my eyes focused on Pete. He's standing in the corner now, and when I'm about ten feet away, he lifts his head and locks eyes with me. I hesitate, Donovan's warning ringing in my ears, but I take a sip of my beer and force my feet to keep moving.

Pete's lips spread into a grin that gets wider the closer I get. Something sinister flashes in his eyes, but it disappears so fast, I think I imagined it.

"You must be Sylvia," Pete says when I stop in front of him.

My stomach flutters at the grit in his voice. It's sexy as hell, and I'm a sucker for a gritty voice. It reminds me of, well, sex.

I tilt my head. "How'd you know my name?" I ask, playing coy while knowing full well he probably just got it from one of the brothers here at the party.

"I asked around," he admits and then drops his voice. "The minute I saw you earlier, I knew I had to have you."

"Ah, a sweet talker." I take another drink of beer. "You must not have asked the right questions then. Because if you had, you'd know that I can't be won over with sweet talk."

Pete leans in and breathes against my ear, sending shivers down my spine. "Nothing about what I want to do to you is sweet."

I grin before pulling away from him.

"Then what are you waiting for?"

Pete grabs my hand and tugs me toward the exit. I glance over my shoulder and see Donovan still at the bar where I left him, and he's watching us. If the stiffness in his body is any indication, he's not happy that I didn't heed his warning. Oh well. Like I told him, I'm a big girl and can take care of myself.

But tonight, I'm going to let Sexy-voice Pete take care of me instead.

When we step outside, Pete slows his walk, forcing me

to do the same because of the grip he has on my hand. It's the kind of grip that feels possessive, feels like I'm the only person to exist around him and he wants to keep me as close as possible.

"I'm over there," he says and points to a BMW parked toward the side of the clubhouse.

Internally, I groan. I would prefer he have a Harley, but I can live with a BMW. If I have to be in a cage, at least it's a nice one.

"Where are we going?" I ask after we're both inside the vehicle.

He starts the engine and grins at me. "I'm taking you for a night you won't ever forget."

"Promise?"

"Oh yeah."

"Good."

I settle into the leather after putting my seat belt on and look out the passenger window. Pete turns on the heater, and he must like it hot because it's on full blast. As the hot air warms me, I realize it feels more like a misty air, and I turn my head to look at Pete. He's got a mask over his mouth and nose, and my stomach bottoms out.

"What's go-oing..." My words slur, and my eyelids grow heavy. I struggle to stay awake, but I don't know how long I can manage it. "W-who are..."

"I promised a night you wouldn't forget," he says from behind the mask. "I'm delivering on that promise."

"Bu..."

My eyes drift closed, and the world goes black.

Chapter Two

It's not about trust. No, it's about me and what I need to do, what I crave.

Trainwreck
Two days later...

I stare at the papers scattered haphazardly on the card table I've set up in what is now my office. It used to be my bedroom, but the bed started getting cluttered with evidence, so I sleep on the couch, unless I'm at the clubhouse.

It's been fourteen years since my sister, Trinity, was taken from my family, and two years since she rose from the dead. The Soulless Kings MC has done a lot to take down the trafficking ring that's responsible for my family's tragedy, and after taking out the leader, Conrad Templeton, they think it's over.

I do not.

"Yo, Trainwreck, where the fuck are you?"

The deep voice startles me, and I whip my head in the direction of the bedroom door. *Dammit!* I race out to the hall, slamming the door shut behind me and coming face to face with Royal. He raises a suspicious brow but pivots and returns to the living room.

"Dude, I knocked like ten times," he grumbles. "What is going on with you?"

I shove a hand through my too long hair and try to come up with a believable answer. "Ah, nothing. Just rearranging the furniture in my bedroom."

Seriously, T, that's the best you can come up with?

"Bullshit." He chuckles.

"Aren't you supposed to be on shift at the gate this morning?"

"I was." He pulls his phone from his pocket, taps the screen, and turns it around so I can see it. "It's two o'clock in the afternoon."

"Fuck!" I race back to my bedroom and search for my own cell phone.

I was supposed to have lunch with Trinity, Greaser, and my nephew, Trenton. We try to get together once a week, and today was the day.

How the fuck did I forget?

The Church of Sinfinite Opportunity, that's how. It's the only thing occupying my mind these days, and—

"Holy shit, bro."

I whirl around to see Royal standing in the doorway, jaw dropped and eyes wide as he takes in the scene before him.

"I don't suppose this can stay between us?"

"Why?" he asks incredulously. "You know the club would back you in taking down more of these pricks."

I nod. "Yeah, I know. But..."

Royal walks to the big bulletin board hanging on the wall and stares at the photos I have tacked to it. There are twenty-three printouts of people who I've managed to connect to the trafficking ring. Fourteen of them have red Xs over their faces, and six of them have no face because I haven't been able to identify them. I only know about their existence because I mapped out connections of other identified individuals by using phone records.

"Have you taken out all of these people by yourself?" Royal asks, pointing toward the board where the majority of the crossed-out faces are.

I stride toward the prospect and clasp a hand on his shoulder. "See, Royal, that's the thing. I'm not sure how to answer that."

He arches a brow.

"On the one hand, if I say 'yes', then I'm guessing you'd be more likely to tell the club because I'm working alone." I shrug. "And if I say 'no', I'd be lying."

"Jesus Christ, T," he mumbles, his head hanging. When he lifts his eyes and looks at me, I know I'm right... This isn't a secret he can keep. "In case you've forgotten, I'm still a prospect. I don't talk, my chances of getting a patch drop to zero."

"And if I ordered you to keep your lips zipped?"

Royal turns and walks back toward the door. Before stepping through, he throws a look over his shoulder. "I'd remind you that you're not my president and your orders carry less weight than our bylaws and everything I know about being a Soulless King."

With that, he disappears into the hallway. A few seconds later, the sound of the front door slamming reverberates through the small house, and I know I'm alone again. No matter... I'm used to being alone. I've been alone since I was nine years old and the ground opened up beneath me, threatening to suck me into a deep abyss.

It did suck you in, but then you met the Soulless Kings. You can trust them.

I shake my head to dislodge the thought. It's not about trust. I trust every single one of my brothers with my life. No, it's about me and what *I* need to do, what *I* crave. Besides, the club thinks the threat is over.

I glance at the board of faces. They couldn't be more fucking wrong.

I run my fingers through my hair and focus on one face. He's the latest individual I've managed to identify, and there's something about him that causes an ice-cold chill to trickle down my spine.

Pete Donaldson.

The only reason he's on the board is because of his connections to the Church. He doesn't have an arrest record. Hell, there's nothing in his background that immediately screams 'evil'. He's even married with three kids. But he's a threat, just the same. Sometimes the bad guys are good at disguising themselves, only letting the evil out when they want. Pete is one of those guys.

And good 'ol Pete's last known location is Portland. In fact, when I trailed him last week, I saw him with a Black Savage. Now what would a man like Pete be doing with an MC? And why in the hell is he in Portland when his family is back in Florida, where he left them a month ago? Nothing adds up.

I shift my eyes to the blank face next to Pete's. The sheer amount of phone calls to whoever this is screams 'connection' to me. One could argue that it's his wife and he misses her, but I have her contact info so I'm able to easily eliminate those calls and avoid going down the wrong rabbit hole.

My muscles tense as I stare at the blank face a few moments longer.

I may not know who you are, but I will figure it out. And then you're—

My phone beeps with an incoming text, causing me to shift gears and search for the device on the table. When I find it under a stack of papers and look at the screen, I freeze.

Fender: Get to the clubhouse… now!

Royal sure didn't waste any time. I scrub a hand over my face as I shove my phone in my pocket, then I race out to the living room. I grab my cut off the back of the couch and put it on as I'm walking out the door. Mental images swirl through my mind as to how this is going to go down.

I could be stripped of my patch.

I search for any other possibility, but I come up empty. No way is this going to go well. I'm done, out of the club… end of story.

The only question now is this: knowing that, does it change anything? Would I do it all again?

In a fucking heartbeat.

Chapter Three

I've never been any good at playing the good little soldier.

Sylvia

"There's someone here to see you."

I can't stop my nose from wrinkling at the sound of Pete's voice outside of the room I'm being held in. Other than my own shouting, demanding to be let go, he's the only person I've heard for the last two days.

Pete's face comes into view, and his fingers curl around the iron bars that make up the doorway. When I woke up in this place two days ago, it was dark, and I was unable to make out the bars. Not that I really tried. It took all the energy I had to wake up and roll over. As time passed and the sun came up to shine through the window, I was able to take in more of my surroundings.

"Did you fucking hear me?"

"Kinda hard not to," I mumble.

I've been in a bedroom and based on the sounds coming from beyond the room, I'm in a house. I've smelled coffee and bacon each morning and dinner cooking each night. I haven't been given any... only bread and water. But there's a bathroom attached to the bedroom, so thank God for that.

Pete's face twists. "How many times do I have to tell you, sarcasm and bitchiness will get you nowhere?"

"I don't know," I snap as I lunge from the edge of the bed toward him, annoyed with his bullshit. "Maybe try a few more and it'll sink in."

Pete rubs his forehead. "Fuck, am I glad you won't be my problem after today." He glares at me. "If you behave."

"What's that supposed to mean?" I demand. "That I won't be your problem after today?"

"It means what it means." He grins and I mentally chastise myself for falling for that grin in the first place.

Pete bends to pick something up, and when he shoves a bag through the bars, I stare at it like it'll burn me if I grab it.

"What is that?" I ask, my eyes narrowed.

"Certainly nothing I'd pick out." Pete leers at me. "If it were up to me, you'd stay in your birthday suit."

I glance down at myself and am reminded that I'm naked. I woke up this way, and Pete's refused to give me anything resembling clothes since. He said it's insurance that I won't run.

Run where?

The windows are built into the walls in a way that makes it impossible to get through them. Trust me, I tried. Besides, it's the middle of winter and there is nothing beyond the windows for as far as the eye could see.

I wrap my arms around myself without giving it a thought. I'd love to stand here and not give a damn about what he sees, but I can't bring myself to do that. I've been with my share of guys, many of them one-night stands, and baring my body never bothered me. But now, with him, it does.

"Take the bag, Sylvia," Pete huffs out as he shakes it.

I reach out and snatch it from his hands, expecting it to burst into flames the second I touch it. When it doesn't, a sigh escapes past my lips and Pete chuckles at the sound.

"Now, get a shower." He nods toward the bathroom. "There's some makeup in the bag, as well as a clean towel and washcloth. You'll also find a toothbrush and anything else you might need." He shoves his hands in his pockets. "You have one hour. Make the most of it."

With those words, he disappears down the hall. After his footsteps cease, I hear voices. Pete's and what sounds like another man's. I strain to make out what they're saying but can't.

After a minute or two, I groan and turn from the door to walk into the bathroom. I take the toiletries out of the bag, along with the towel, which I drape over the bar on the wall. I'm surprised at the fluffiness of it. It's plush and nothing like what I'd expect from good ol' Pete.

Next, I pull out the remaining contents. I set the makeup on the counter, and my jaw drops at the dress and heels in the bottom of the bag. I hang the dress on the door and take a step back to stare at it. It's black with a deep plunging neckline and absolutely no back to speak of. The dress is long, and the heels are tall.

Who the fuck is here to see me, and why in the hell do they want me to wear this?

Pushing the thought aside, I step into the shower and turn the water to as hot a temperature as I can stand. I scrub my body free of two days' worth of grime. It could be worse, I suppose. At least I haven't been out in the elements. If I had, there'd be a lot more filth swirling around the drain.

I take my time in the shower, savoring the normalcy of it. When I'm done, I towel myself dry and look around for a hair dryer. Realizing there isn't one, I tsk a few times. Something tells me this little oversight of Pete's isn't going to turn out well for him. I glance at the dress. Anyone who wants a woman to wear that surely doesn't want them in it with straggly wet hair.

I wrap the towel around my head and get dressed. Everything fits like a glove. I study myself in the mirror and realize that, under other circumstances, I'd love this dress. It's beautiful really. The perfect amount of classy mixed with sexy. It accentuates my curves, highlights my cleavage, makes me feel like a prin—

My fist connects with the mirror, and glass shatters, shards of it either falling into the sink or sticking out of my knuckles. Blood swirls with it, creating a weird sort of art in the porcelain bowl. I hiss at the pain in my hand as I gently remove pieces of glass, running my hand under water with each sliver added to the art collection.

As I'm rinsing my hand, I hear the bars on the door to the bedroom being opened, and within seconds, an insistent banging rattles the bathroom door.

"Open the door, Sylvia," Pete demands.

I hang my head and let my hands fall to my sides, not giving a shit about the blood that drips onto the floor.

"Why did you punch the mirror?" he asks, and I whip my head up and around to glare at the door.

How the hell does he know that? I lift my eyes to the corners of the ceiling, and that's when I see it, a camera. How did I miss that?

Pete continues to pound on the barrier, each bang more

insistent than the last. My temples begin to throb. I ignore the blooming headache and reach for the door to turn the lock. The door is immediately shoved open, and I have to step back to avoid being hit with it.

Pete takes in the scene before him, his face twisting more and more with each passing glance.

"Jesus, you can't make things easy, can you?" he barks. I shake my head. "Too late now. Hopefully you'll be accepted in as-is condition."

His words travel through my brain, but they don't make sense. Not only do I have a headache, but now my head is spinning as I continue to lose blood, which is making it hard to concentrate.

"What is the meaning of this?"

I snap my head up and look beyond Pete to see a man standing behind him. I don't recognize him, but that doesn't surprise me. He's wearing a black suit, tailored to fit him perfectly, and an angry scowl.

Pete's face drains of all color as he slowly turns to face the man. His shoulders slump, and in seconds, he's no longer the confident asshole who gassed me and held me captive. Shifting my eyes between the two men, I'm not sure if the addition of the new guy is a good thing or not. Something tells me he's not here to rescue me.

"I'm sorry, sir," Pete says pathetically. "She's been a handful."

A handful? I haven't done a damn thing.

"And why is that, Peter?" the other guy asks. "Is it because you're not cut out for the job?" He reaches behind his back and pulls a gun from his waistband. He points it at Pete's head. "Because that's the only thing that makes sense." He pulls back the hammer with his thumb. "How hard is it to beat a girl into submission? Two days was plenty of time."

"Sir, if you'll let me explain... Sylvia isn't just any—"

"Sylvia?"

"Yes, Sylvia, Black Savages MC princess," Pete clarifies.

The man pistol whips Pete. "You fucking moron! I paid for the princess, not the little sister, the nobody of the club."

"Wait," I demand, although it doesn't come out as forcefully as I want it to. "First, I'm not a nobody. And second, if you were looking for Charlie," I nod toward Pete. "This douchebag went to the wrong club."

"Is she right, Peter?"

"No!"

The man swivels his head between the two of us, squinting as if he's trying to figure out who to believe. When the gun goes off and blood and goo splatters across my face, all over the room really, I know he believes me.

As he bends to reach over Pete's slumped body for my discarded towel, his eyes never leave me. He stands back up and wipes off his gun before tucking it back into his waistband.

"I suppose I should introduce myself," he says casually.

I simply stand there, rooted in place. It's not that I haven't seen violence, or even been a part of it. I'm used to blood and coldhearted pricks. But this guy, in his fancy suit, with his perfectly styled hair... he's something different.

"I'm Bob."

I can't stop the snort that bursts from me, but at Bob's look of derision, I quickly sober.

"Is my name funny to you?"

I shake my head. "No, not funny. But it's also not your real name."

"And you know this how?"

I shrug. "Just do."

"Whether or not Bob is my real name is irrelevant." He glances at Pete for a second before returning cold eyes to me. "I may have paid for your sister, but you're who I'm stuck with. I'm all you've got in this world, so you'll do as you're told."

I open my mouth to argue, but Bob backhands me across the face. My cheek stings and it's another level of pain to add to my ever-growing list.

"What was that for?" I snarl.

"Let's go," he demands, ignoring my question entirely.

"No, not until you tell me where we're going."

"Little girl, if you think that bit of information will do you any good, you're sadly mistaken." Bob turns his back on me. "Now, let's go."

I watch as he walks away, out of the bedroom and into the hall, no doubt believing that I'm following him. He's the one who's *sadly mistaken* if he thinks I'll blindly follow like some lemming.

I remain where I am for several minutes, expecting him to reappear any moment. When he does, I almost wish I'd followed him.

He stalks toward me. I take in the black coat he's now wearing over his suit, as well as the gun in his hand. It's pointed at my head, and it takes everything in me not to flinch.

When Bob reaches me, he presses the barrel of the gun to my forehead.

"We can do this the easy way or the hard way. Up to you."

"I choose door number two."

My brain screams at me to quit taunting him, to shut my

mouth and do what I'm told, but I've never been any good at playing the good little soldier.

"So *Bob*, do you have what it takes to do things the hard way or are you just as big a pussy as Pete?"

Rather than respond, Bob swings his arm and hits me over the head with the butt of the pistol.

More pain reverberates through my skull for a millisecond before I fall to the floor in an unconscious heap.

Chapter Four

I need to focus on the anger because that's what's going to get me through this.

Trainwreck

"You know you're lucky you're still here, right?"

I lift my head up and stare at Greaser across the table. We're waiting for the others to arrive for our third session of church in the last two days. We got an emergency text from Fender this morning, but Greaser asked me to come early, so here we are.

"Yeah." I nod slowly. "Yeah, I know."

"Why the fuck wouldn't you come to me with everything you had?" he demands, not for the first time. "I'm married to your sister for Christ's sake. I have a stake in this."

"You don't think I know that?!" I shout, shooting up from my chair to pace the room. "I know exactly who this affects and what's at stake. I'm not the idiot who showed up here a few years ago."

"I know that, T," Greaser agrees. "Which is what makes this even more frustrating. You know better."

I stop pacing when I reach my chair and bend to rest my hands on the table. Leaning across it a bit, I ask, "Have you told Trinity about any of this yet?"

"What do you think?" he huffs out.

"He doesn't think." I whirl toward the door and see Fender tossing his weapons into the box. "That's the fucking problem."

Piston walks in behind Fender. "Oh, I don't know about that. I think he thought about a lot of things. The club just wasn't one of them."

And so it goes as all the brothers show up within a few minutes. Each one takes their shot at me, angry that I acted alone but not *so* angry that I'll lose my patch. I know I have to prove myself to them again, show that they can trust me, but that's easy. To do that, all I have to do is finish what I started with the Church of Sinfinite Opportunity... with the club's help.

"We need to get started so sit the fuck down!" Piston shouts as he bangs the gavel.

"Did. You. Tell. Her?" I ask Greaser again as I sit.

"Of course I told her," he seethes.

"Are you two finished?" Fender barks. "Because we've got shit to do."

Both Greaser and I clamp our lips shut and shift our focus to our president.

"Jesus, maybe I *should* have taken away your patch."

"Prez, that won't be—"

Fender raises a hand to cut me off. "Don't, Trainwreck."

I lean back in my chair and make a conscious effort not to cross my arms over my chest and huff out a breath. All that would do is make me look like a child throwing a tantrum, and that's the last thing I need.

When it's finally quiet, Fender begins Church.

"Does anyone need us to review the information we've discussed the last two sessions?" he asks.

Those sessions focused on all the information I've gathered: names, locations, connections, phone numbers... everything.

I look around the room to see how each man responds, fully expecting to have to explain something, but they all shake their heads.

"Good." Fender pulls his phone out of his pocket and taps the screen before setting it down on the table. "Now we can get to this." He dips his head to talk into the cell. "Donovan, you still there?"

Donovan? The president of the Black Savages?

I sit up a little straighter

"Damn, Fender, took you long enough," Donovan bites out. "Next time, don't call me until your crew is actually ready."

Fender scowls. "You're the one who texted me this morning, demanding I call an emergency church session because you need our help with something. Do you want it or not?"

A long sigh comes through the line. "Unfortunately, I *need* it, so yeah, I want it."

"That's what I thought," Fender counters, his voice tight. "Now, fill us in."

"Three days ago, we had a party at the clubhouse," he begins. "Nothing out of the ordinary. Booze, pot, sex, music... just the normal blowing off steam."

"I'm going to go ahead and assume that the night was anything *normal*," Piston says.

Ignoring the jibe, Donovan continues. "There were a few people there who I didn't recognize, but that's typical. Brothers invite chicks, friends. We have an open-door policy for some of our parties." He takes a deep breath, blows it out. "Anyway, there was one guy there who I knew was bad news. Sylvia set her—"

"What the fuck?!" Fender shouts. "You didn't say this had to do with Sylvia. She's family, you prick. Don't you think you should have started with that?"

"I know she's family," Donovan concedes hotly. "To all of us."

"Goddamnit," Fender mumbles. "You've got two minutes to get to the point."

"It won't take that long."

"What's that supposed to mean?"

"Sylvia has been missing since that night."

The table rattles when Fender punches it. He thrusts stiff hands through his hair and begins to pace, seemingly unable to contain the fury roaring in him.

"What does the guy you say is bad news have to do with Sylvia missing?" I ask, thoughts swirling in my mind.

My muscles are tense as I wait for Donovan to answer. I don't know why, but my gut tells me I'm not going to like his answer… or maybe it'll be exactly what I need.

"Sylvia left with him."

Donovan proceeds to tell us how Sylvia and Brick have been seeing each other, but that night, she turned him away because he was being a dick. He explains how she set her sights on this guy, and, despite Donovan's warnings, left with him.

"What's the guy's name?" I ask.

"Pete." Donovan pauses for a second. "I know his last name but can't think of —"

"Donaldson," I spit out, my stomach dropping.

"Yeah, Donaldson," Donovan confirms. "How'd you know that?"

"Because," Fender begins, not giving me a chance to respond. "He's been going solo on a trafficking ring, and Pete Donaldson is the next person in his kill line."

"You have no idea just how *bad news* Pete is," I snarl. "Why did you wait this long to call us?"

Donovan doesn't respond.

"I'd like to know the answer to that, too," Fender says. "You know how Charlie is, and when I tell her that her sister is missing, for three days no less, things are gonna get ugly."

"Look, Sylvia has really blossomed since Charlie married your sorry ass," Donovan finally says. "I don't think she's told Charlie the half of what she's dealt with since she left, but I've watched Sylvia deal with one thing after another. She was finally happy again… or maybe for the first time in her life, I don't know. Either way, I'm not her father. I'm her friend, and all I can do is watch out for her. I did that."

"Apparently not," Fender snorts.

"Do you really think I don't blame myself?!" Donovan yells. "Because I do. I've been playing the what ifs in my head, over and over. It doesn't help. At the end of the day, I can't change what happened or what I did. What I can do is find her and bring her home. Now, can you help me do that or not?"

Rather than answer Donovan, Fender looks at me. "T, do you have enough to track Pete down?"

"Almost." I scrub my hands over my face. "I'll need some help and all the information the Black Savages have on him."

"Done," Donovan says. "I'll bring it over as soon as I hang up."

"Okay. T, I want you to be in charge of this." When I open my mouth to speak, Fender holds his hand up to stop me. "This is not a reward for all your hard solo work. But you know more than any of us about the Church of Sinfinite Opportunity and the man, or men, we're going to hunt down." Fender scans the room. "All those in favor of Trainwreck running the show, thump twice."

The only brother who doesn't give two thumps is Squirrel. Honestly, I understand his hesitation. He's the tech guy of the club and is crucial in everything we do. He can track people better than anyone I know. But he doesn't know the Church like I do.

"Done," Fender says. "Donovan, get your info over here, and we'll go from there."

"I'm bringing a few of my guys with me. The more eyes on this, the better."

Fender glances at me, and I shrug. I don't care who helps at this point. As long as the end result is getting Sylvia home and the Church taken down, I'm good.

"Fine, see you soon."

Fender taps his phone to end the call and finally sits down. He scowls as he takes in everyone around the table.

"This is not something we can fuck up, got it?"

"Got it." The words echo through the space.

"Good. Head over to Trainwreck's house, and I'll send Donovan when he gets here." Fender stands again. "Now if you'll excuse me, I've gotta go tell my wife that her sister's missing."

Fender disappears from the room, and the rest of the brothers slowly file out behind him. I remain in my chair for a few moments, absorbing what is happening. The more I think, the more my rage builds until it feels like it's going to burn me up from the inside out.

Like Donovan, the what ifs begin to play in my mind, and I shove them aside. I need to focus on the anger because that's what's going to get me through this. That's what will keep me on track, like a dog with a bone.

That anger is what will bring Sylvia home.

Chapter Five

That would resurrect the devil in him for sure.

Sylvia

"Time to get up."

A deluge of cold water sloshes over my head, and I jackknife into a sitting position. I press my fists against my eyes before swiping water away from my face. When my fingers reach my hairline, I wince as they touch the knot.

"Not so lippy now, are you?"

I lift my head and glare at Bob. The smirk on his face taunts me to argue, but I refrain. That's what he wants, and I refuse to give him anything he wants.

"Now that you're awake, I can show you to your room," he tells me, reaching out his hand to help me stand. "I believe you'll find your accommodations are much better than where you were previously."

I ignore his offered hand and rise to my feet. I sway and Bob grabs a hold of my shoulders to steady me.

"Easy now," he croons and nods at my forehead where he hit me with the butt of his gun. "No need to add more damage."

I shake free of his hold, and he grins. Smug bastard.

"Where are we?" I ask, trying not to let my voice shake.

Bob is now my second captor, and I'm beginning to worry. I thought for sure the Black Savages would have found me by now, especially since Donovan seemed to know Pete. Hell, my sister has to know I'm missing so the Soulless Kings should have been here, too. I have two motorcycle clubs looking out for me. How the hell am I that hard to find?

"Does it matter?"

To me it does, but I hesitate to say that. For some reason, Bob doesn't seem to be as concerned with my possible escape or rescue, and there's no need for me to bring it to his attention. The longer I'm held in one place, the easier it'll be for someone to find me.

Realizing I've been silent for too long, I shrug. "Guess not."

"Good." He turns toward the door, glancing over his shoulder when he reaches it. "Coming?"

Without giving me a chance to respond, he continues out the door, and I follow. Time to see my accommodations.

As he walks me through the house—more like an ornately decorated mansion—I make mental notes of any potential escape routes. We follow a long, curved hallway until we reach the end. There's no doorway or any visible exit from the hallway, except to go back the way we came.

I look over my shoulder and see nothing but deep red walls and ugly sconces providing very dim lighting. When I return my gaze forward, I see Bob pull down on the one and only sconce in front of him. A hidden door swings open, and the reinforced steel behind the gaudy wallpaper becomes visible.

Bob reaches for my hand and grabs it to practically drag me down a set of winding steps. The farther down we go, the colder it gets, until the stairwell opens up into what appears to be a small version of an open concept apartment... with cinder block walls and a concrete floor.

I yank out of his hold. "I thought you said my accommodations would be better," I grit out.

Bob turns in a circle, almost as if he's trying to determine why I'm unhappy. When he faces me, there's a sinister grin lifting his lips. "I did, and they are."

"Hardly," I scoff.

"You have a bit more space," he points out. "Besides, I didn't say who the accommodations were better for, did I?" He quirks a brow at me before continuing. "No, I did not. Now, I think you'll find that they *are* better, *for me*. You might as well forget any plans of escaping. You can't. And being rescued? Not possible. There is nothing that can penetrate these walls. No windows, no hint that there's even a basement underground." His grin slips for a second, but he recovers quickly. "You might not be who I wanted, but you're who I got. I plan to make the best of it. I suggest you do the same."

A shiver races down my spine at the way his voice lowers with his last few words. I force my eyes away from him, needing to look at anything but Bob. I don't know what he has planned for me, but it can't be good.

"We'll see about that," I mumble.

My scalp stings when he threads his fingers in my hair and yanks my face toward him. I try to disengage from him, but he's stronger than he appears.

"What did you say?" Bob snarls.

"Nothing."

He yanks harder. "I'm going to let you in on a little secret." Bob drags me toward the bed and throws me face down onto it. "I don't like liars."

I flip over and scoot toward the wall. The brick is cold on my bare back, but I ignore it. "Not many people do."

"I see we're back to being lippy."

"I can't help it."

Bob tilts his head to the side as if evaluating the truth in my statement. Finally, he crosses the room and stops at the bottom of the stairwell.

"Learn to control it," he says without looking at me. "It'll make your life easier."

Bob takes his cell phone out of his pocket and presses a button. Loud classical music fills the room. He disappears up the steps, and the door at the top shuts with a bang.

Great... just fucking great.

As if this whole situation weren't bad enough, I have to suffer through it with this bullshit playing in my ears?

I ROLL OVER ON THE BED AND PRETEND THAT THERE'S sun streaming through a window. There's not of course... no windows. But after being stuck in this prison, pretending is the only thing getting me through.

I glance at the nightstand and count the pieces of string I've laid out to keep track of how long I've been here.

Twelve.

Twelve motherfucking days in hell.

Every night before I go to sleep, I pull a strand from the blanket on the bed. It took me a while to get the edge frayed enough to do this, but it kept my mind occupied, so I can't complain.

Twelve days of being used like some sort of sex toy.

Twelve days of being fed the best foods in an effort to make me think this is some sort of gift I've been given.

Twelve days and twelve different dresses, each more beautiful than the last and each making me feel cheaper than the one before it.

Twelve days of this motherfucking classical music burning through my ear drums. Give me AC/DC, Metallica, Def Leppard, or even country, any day of the week and I'm good. Classical music only makes me want to shove an ice pick into my ears to stop any and all sound from getting in.

"Rise and shine," Bob's voice beams from the loudspeaker, the only reprieve from the music I ever get.

I swing my legs over the edge of the bed and plant my feet on the floor. The first few days, the cold of the concrete was a shock to my system, but Bob took pity on me and now I have a rug.

Pulling at the blanket to wrap it around my naked body, I cringe when I hear Bob again.

"Ah, ah, ahh. You know the rules."

I heave a sigh and shrug the blanket off.

The rules. I'm so sick of the goddamn rules. Eat the food provided, wear the dress I'm given until bedtime, always sleep naked, and never cower from Bob when he comes to me. No matter what he does or asks me to do, I'm to obey. I've learned the hard way how much of a stickler for rules Bob is.

The one saving grace, if I follow the rules, is being permitted outside... for thirty minutes and with a guard of course. Oh, and let's not forget the cage I have to stay in. It reminds me of what real prisoners are let loose in when they have yard time. But even they get an hour.

"Today's dress is hanging in the bathroom, ready for you."

I glance at the speaker in the corner of the ceiling across from me and debate flipping it off. I don't know if there's a camera next to it or not, but there are cameras somewhere in this hole and Bob would get the gist. I decide against it in the interest of avoiding his wrath.

The music comes back on, and I know I have approximately forty-five minutes to get ready before the steel door opens and Bob arrives.

I stand and walk to the bathroom, my feet dragging and my body sluggish. After not sleeping the first few nights, Bob started giving me a sedative at bedtime to ensure I get enough sleep to be alert and engaging when he's with me. Bastard. Unfortunately, he doesn't know shit about proper dosing, and it takes a cold shower to wash away the last of the effects in the morning.

Time seems to pass faster than usual, and just as I'm stepping out of the bathroom, clad in the dress, makeup and hair perfectly done, Bob steps off the last step.

"You look beautiful today," he quips with a smile on his face.

This is why this man is so dangerous. He flips from charming to evil as fast as I can snap my fingers. I never know which I'm going to get, unless I break one of the rules.

"Thank you," I respond, as expected.

He walks across the room toward me, stopping when he can reach out and touch my cheek. When he caresses it, it's all I can do not to cringe or pull away from him. That would resurrect the devil in him for sure.

"Are you hungry this morning?" he asks as he wraps his hand around the back of my neck to pull me closer.

I shake my head.

"I'll have Ramon make you a big lunch then."

"That would be nice."

He drops his arm and takes a step back. His hands go to his belt buckle, and he undoes that before shoving his pants over his hips so they can fall and pool around his ankles.

Bob grins and lets the evil take over.

"Shall we begin?"

Chapter Six

I'm glad you're alive.

Trainwreck

"What the fuck are you waiting for?"

I look at Fender and Charlie out of the corner of my eye as I pretend my attention is still on the map in front of me. They've been arguing for the last twelve days. Charlie is full of so much pain and anger, both of which I understand completely. But I wish she'd stop taking it out on Fender. It isn't his fault her sister is missing. It's not on him that it took us this long to track her down.

Fender's lips move, but I can't make out what he's saying. Whatever it is, it's not the right thing because Charlie slaps him across the face and races from the room.

Fender goes after her, but I rush to stop him at the door.

"Let me talk to her, Prez," I say, my palm flat against his chest.

He glances at my hand and then lifts his eyes to scowl at me. "She's my wife," he snarls.

I drop my arm. "Fender, listen to me." His scowl deepens, and I know I'm pushing it. But I don't let that deter me. "I've been in Charlie's shoes before. I know exactly how she's feeling. Just... give me a few minutes to see if I can calm her down."

Fender draws in a deep breath before blowing it out and hanging his head. He runs a hand through his hair and then looks at me.

"Fine. But if you make things worse..."

I put my hands up in mock surrender. "Got it."

I turn from him and race into the main room of the clubhouse. I glance around for Charlie and see her sitting at the bar, an empty shot glass in front of her. Margo is standing behind the bar, a worried look on her face.

I close the distance between us and sit on the stool next to Charlie.

"Trainwreck, I'm not in the mood to talk," she says hotly and without looking at me.

"That's fine," I say and lift a finger to Margo to let her know I'll take a shot. "You don't have to talk. But will you please listen?"

She glares at me.

"Please?" I ask. "Fender will kill me if I upset you, so don't sign my death warrant."

"Whatever," she snaps before gesturing to Margo to pour her another.

I toss my shot back, savoring the burn as the liquid travels through me. It's the only liquor I'm going to get today because I have to remain sharp for tonight.

"I know the last two weeks have been hell for you. If anyone knows exactly what you've been through, it's me."

Charlie slowly shifts her gaze to me, and her eyes well up with tears. I want to reach out and give her a hug because that's what I wish someone would have done for me. I want to comfort her and ease her burden. But I can feel Fender's eyes boring a hole in the back of my head from the hallway. If he thinks he's being sneaky or that I didn't expect him to keep an eye on his wife, he's mistaken.

"How did you get through it?" she asks me when I remain silent a beat too long.

"I prospected for an MC," I say on a hollow laugh. "Lucky for you, you already have two surrounding you."

"Yeah, but when you were little, how did you do it? How did you not die a little each day that Trinity was gone?"

"I didn't die a little each day. I died a thousand times between the day she was taken and the day I got her back. I killed the little boy I was and returned an angry, bitter adult."

"This isn't helping, T."

"It would if you'd let it," I say to her. "It helps to talk to someone who understands. I'm not going to tell you what to think, feel, or even how to act." I sigh, sure I'm fucking this up. "I just want you to know I'm here and I get it."

"You don't get it," she bites out. "I don't want you here! I want you out there." She points toward the door. "I want you and everyone else to get on your goddamn bikes and go get Sylvia. I want her back!"

"And we will, Charlie." I push her arm down slowly. "But you know as well as I do that we have to wait until tonight. You've been a part of this search every step of the way. You know how well this guy has hidden her. We have a plan, and it's a damn good one. You know it."

"Doesn't mean I have to like it," she huffs out.

"You're right, you don't," I agree.

Charlie runs her fingers through her hair and spins on the stool to face me fully. "I miss her so damn much, ya know? I mean, we may not have always been close, and it's no secret that I don't like all of her life choices, but she's my sister. Whether or not we talk every day or hang out on a regular basis, she'll always be my sister... my baby sister."

"I know." I glance over my shoulder and give a single nod in Fender's direction. He starts walking toward us, and I return my eyes to Charlie. "But can you try to give Fender a break? He loves you, and Sylvia, and not being able to fix this... it's killing him too."

Charlie shifts her focus to her husband when he reaches us, and her face falls even more. "Jesus, Fender, I'm sorry. I'm not trying to take it out on you."

Fender wraps an arm around Charlie and pulls her to her feet and into his chest. "I know."

I start to walk away, suddenly feeling like I'm intruding on a very private moment, but Fender stops me in my tracks.

"Trainwreck?"

I look back at him. "Yeah?"

"Thanks."

"No problem." I grin. "And Prez?"

"Yeah?"

"We ride at midnight."

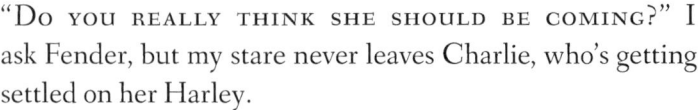

"Do you really think she should be coming?" I ask Fender, but my stare never leaves Charlie, who's getting settled on her Harley.

"Do you want to be the one to tell her she can't?" Fender counters.

"Fuck no." I chuckle, but it holds little amusement. "Look, I know she's more than capable of handling herself, but she needs to stick to the back. I don't want anything to happen to her or for her to fuck shit up because she's too emotionally invested."

"Watch it, T," Fender warns. "You may be in charge of this mission, but I'm still your president and she's still my wife. She'll be fine."

"Understood."

I mount my Harley, and once we're all ready, I lead the brothers off Soulless Kings property and in the direction of Northern California. We have about a two-hour ride, both ways, and a dangerous plan. It's going to be a long night.

Two and a half hours later, we pull to the side of the road, just past the mansion we tracked Sylvia to. Once we found Pete, dead in his home, we started tracking his killer and going back through his phone records. It didn't take long to find Bartholomew Jones. Finding his location is what took the majority of our time.

"Are you sure this is it?" Piston asks as he walks up to me.

Squirrel joins him. "We're sure."

Squirrel is actually the one who tracked Bartholomew here, through property records. Then he hacked the security system, and that's when we discovered that drones are used to monitor the outside. And that's when we confirmed that Sylvia is here.

We saw her in a cage one day, and after watching several days' worth of footage, it became clear she's only taken outside once a day. Black Savage's MC wanted to go in and grab her during one of those times, but I vetoed that pretty quickly. Bartholomew is smart. We need the element of surprise that the cover of darkness allows us.

"Anyone have any questions about the plan?" I ask, glancing from one brother to the next, one club to the other. When all of the Soulless Kings and Black Savages shake their heads, I continue. "Great. For those of you heading toward the south end of the structure, get your supplies ready. Fender, Joker, Greaser, and I will head to the cage. The rest of you, and Charlie, surround the house and nab Bartholomew and anyone else who comes out. I don't care if you kill others," I focus my gaze on Charlie. "But Bartholomew is to be taken alive. When your task is complete, get the fuck out of there. We'll meet back at the Soulless Kings' clubhouse at." I glance around at everyone. "Let's roll."

We all go in our respective directions. It doesn't take more than ten minutes before fire alarms pierce the air, and a blaze of flames are seen at the south side of the mansion. Fender, Joker, Greaser and I are surrounding the cage, waiting for Sylvia to be led there.

When no one appears outside for several minutes, my anxiety kicks up a bit. What if I'm wrong? What if Bartholomew leaves Sylvia inside? What if everyone stays inside?

I shake my head free of its traitorous thoughts. No, I'm not wrong. I can't be wrong.

And if I am, I'll go in and get Sylvia myself.

Two minutes later, I breathe a sigh of relief when I hear panicked voices. I train my eyes on the door that Sylvia is typically led from when she's put in the cage. It's another minute before I spot her, slung over a man's shoulder and wrapped in a blanket, being carried like a sack of potatoes. We all tighten the perimeter around the metal container she's dumped in. The man leaves her there and starts to return to the mansion. A single gunshot fires, and he drops to the ground.

There are no doors to the chain link cage. Hell, it's even got a matching roof, so there's no climbing over a side to get to Sylvia. I pull out my wire cutters and start working my way in.

More gunfire sounds as I feverishly cut the chain link. Everyone has strict orders not to kill Bartholomew, and I can only pray they're following them.

I shove the sounds and my surroundings out of my mind and focus on the woman who's stirring only twenty-five feet away from me. When she was first brought out, she wasn't moving, and I'd be lying if it didn't cross my mind that we were too late. But now, now that she's moving and I can hear her quiet moans, another flood of relief swirls through my body.

"Sylvia," I call to her. "I need you to get up. Can you do that for me?"

Her head turns my way, and she squints as if trying to make out who's talking to her. The only light we have is from the flames as they tear through the house like a knife slices through warm butter.

"Who's there?" she asks, her voice scratchy and sounding groggy.

I cut through the last link and climb through the hole to jog toward her. When I get close, she tries to scoot away, but she's too slow. I bend to lift her in my arms because she doesn't seem to be able to stand... or she doesn't want to.

She thrashes against my hold, pounds my chest, kicks her legs wildly. She's scared, so her behavior doesn't surprise me, but we don't have time for it. I need to get her out of here.

"Get her under control!" Fender yells at me. "We have to get out of here."

Sylvia's movements slow, and she frantically shifts her gaze to find the source of Fender's voice.

"Fender?" She wraps her arms around me like a monkey and pulls herself to where she can see beyond my head. "Fender is that you?"

"Yes, Syl, it is," he confirms, his voice softer. "You need to calm down so Trainwreck can get you out of that cage. Can you do that?"

Sylvia nods and squeaks out a quiet 'yes'.

"Good," Fender says. "As soon as you're out of there, we'll get to the bikes and get you home."

"O-okay."

Sylvia finally relaxes in my arms and rests her head on my shoulder. I carry her out through the hole, careful not to scrape her up too badly as we pass through the wires. When we're free of her own personal prison, she breathes deeply and tightens her hold around my neck.

"He was gonna let me burn," she mumbles.

I continue to carry her in the direction of the Harleys, but my muscles tense at her words. Fender, Joker, and Greaser surround us to make sure we're not being followed.

"Who was going to let you burn?" I ask, sure I know the answer already.

"Bob."

Who the fuck is Bob?

"But one of the guards took pity on me after hearing me scream," she says. "I don't remember which one because he hit me in the head to knock me out, but I'd be ash if it weren't for him."

I shift one hand to feel around her head for a wound, and my fingers come back sticky when I get to the left side of her hairline around her face. Rage wraps around me like a boa constrictor killing its prey. I try to break free of the emotion, but the harder I try, the more it constricts.

"I'm glad you're alive," I say, knowing the words probably mean nothing to her, but needing to say something.

Sylvia lifts her head and looks me in the eye, causing me to stop walking for a moment.

"What is it?" I ask, when she doesn't say anything.

The tiniest smile lifts her lips.

"Me too, Trainwreck. Me too."

Chapter Seven

I get to out-evil the devil.

Sylvia

"You can't stay in here forever."

I wind my hands through the bathwater but make no move to lift my head to look at Charlie. When we first arrived at the Soulless Kings' clubhouse, there was a heated argument about whether or not I should return to the Black Savages MC, to my home. The majority of the club thought I should, but Charlie dug in her heels, so here I am... in her and Fender's house, in their bathtub, trying to soak away some of the last two weeks.

"I know."

But shit it would be nice if I could.

Charlie paces the bathroom, her bare feet slapping against the tiled floor. After several minutes of this, I lift my head and glare at her.

"Can you stop?" I snap. I throw my hands up and fling water through the air.

It does the trick. Charlie stops in her tracks and crosses her arms over her chest, glaring at me the entire time.

"Was that necessary?" she asks with a bite in her tone.

I shrug. "It worked, didn't it?"

My sister huffs out a breath and shakes her head. "I don't know why I thought you'd be—"

A knock on the door cuts her off. We both swivel our heads to look at the barrier.

"What?" Charlie snips.

"Fender wants you both back at the clubhouse."

I recognize the voice as Trainwreck's and dip lower into the water. When he carried me away from the mansion, I had the blanket as cover, but now, I feel vulnerable in the way Bob made me feel... exposed and disgustingly vulnerable.

"Tell him we'll be there when we get there," Charlie responds.

"C'mon, Charlie, you know I can't do that." Trainwreck rattles the doorknob. "Besides, we've got Bartholomew in the Nightmare Room, and you said you wanted—"

Charlie reaches out and yanks the door open. It takes a split second for my arms to listen to my brain and snatch the towel off the toilet seat and cover myself. It takes a few seconds longer for me to register that the towel is now as wet as I am because I'm still under water.

Trainwreck pushes past Charlie and grabs another towel off the shelf.

"Jesus, why the hell would you open the door when she's in here naked?" Trainwreck extends a hand toward me. "Do you have any idea what she's been through?"

Charlie shuffles her feet, sufficiently chastised for her action. "No, because she won't talk to me. But you don't either, T."

Trainwreck whirls on Charlie. "She was naked under that blanket when she was dumped in the cage. That tells me all I need to know." When he turns toward me, his face softens, and he extends his hand again. "Can you stand up for me Sylvia? I won't see anything because of the towel."

His eyes remain locked on mine, and I stare into them, mesmerized by the truth and conviction in them. I've known Trainwreck for several years now, ever since Charlie and Fender got back together. He's always been a horny little fuck, but I don't see any of that right now. And if it's there, he's hiding it well.

No, the Trainwreck standing before me is the same person I've always known, and at the same time, so very different. He's older, for one, more muscular, chiseled. And he's gentler, kinder, wiser. He's not such a, well, train wreck. I've noticed the changes in him over the years but never were they quite so apparent as they are in this moment.

I settle my hand in his and let him help me stand. Charlie huffs and mumbles something unintelligible before disappearing from the room.

My shoulders slump.

Trainwreck helps me replace the wet towel with the dry one and then slips a finger under my chin.

"You know she loves you, right?"

"She's got a funny way of showing it sometimes."

"Maybe," Trainwreck concedes. "But the love is always there."

He drops his arm to his side and finally breaks eye contact before returning to the doorway.

"I'll let you get dressed," he says. "And then we really do need to get to the clubhouse."

He leaves the room, pulling the door shut behind him.

When he's gone, I bend to pull the stopper and watch as the water recedes lower and lower in the tub until it spirals around the drain and disappears.

When I straighten, I catch a glimpse of myself in the mirror and cringe. It's not that I didn't notice how awful and bruised I was back in my concrete *accommodations*, but there was always the makeup and dresses to compensate for it. I glance down at the counter. Now all I have are the sweats Charlie left for me.

I rifle through the drawers to see if there's any makeup, or at least foundation, to cover all the ugliness, and I find nothing. It shouldn't surprise me. It's not like Charlie set me up in their big bathroom. I'm in the smaller one off the hallway. She wouldn't keep all her toiletries and shit in here.

After quickly drying off, I throw on the green sweats and matching hoodie and call it good. When I enter the living room, Trainwreck is sitting on the couch, looking at his phone. He sees me and stands, turning his cell so I can see it.

Fender: Come straight to the Nightmare Room

"What are we going there for?" I ask,

I'm familiar with the Nightmare Room as far as knowing what the Soulless Kings use it for. It's an interrogation room, a torture chamber... a kill site. I've never been in it, but I've heard the stories. So many fucking stories.

"That's where Bartholomew is?"

"Who's Bartholomew?" I ask, my nose scrunched as I try to recall the name.

Trainwreck's expression shows surprise. "What do you mean? He's the guy who took you."

"Oh," I mumble. "So that's his real name." I lock eyes with Trainwreck. "He called himself Bob."

"That's who you were talking about back at the mansion, as we were leaving."

I nod.

"Well then, Bob is in the Nightmare Room. And you're gonna get a go at him."

My eyes widen, and suddenly, my anxiety disappears and is replaced by a weird sort of excitement.

I get to exact revenge for the last two weeks.

I get to let out all the rage and pain and emotion Bob made me feel.

I get to out-evil the devil.

Chapter Eight

All we can do is take care of business and move forward.

Trainwreck

I can't stop looking at Sylvia out of the corner of my eye as we walk to the back entrance of the Nightmare Room. When she came out of the bathroom earlier, I almost swallowed my tongue. I've always thought she was beautiful, but there's something about natural beauty, void of makeup, and the way she looks in sweats that's... adorable and very appealing.

"Remind me again why I can't just kill him when we get there?"

I stop in my tracks and turn to step in front of her. She squares her shoulders, and it reminds me of the woman she's always been, full of fire and spirit, the one who stands up for herself and doesn't conform to what others expect from her. This side of her, mixed with the adorableness of the sweats and vulnerability, is intoxicating.

"If you can't keep your temper under control, I won't be allowed to let you in the room."

She shoves me with outstretched arms. "My temper?" she argues. "I think after what I've been through, I'm allowed to be a bit pissed off."

I rest my hands on her shoulders, and she relaxes... slightly. "Syl, listen to me."

I stare at her until she agrees. It takes a minute or two, but eventually she dips her head in a nod.

"We can't kill Bartholomew." I gently cover her mouth when she opens it to protest. "I know you want to. Fuck, *I* want to. We all want to. But we can't. Not if we want any chance of taking down the Church."

She narrows her eyes, and when I feel her lips move behind my hand, I lower it so she can speak.

"First, don't ever do that again," she snaps. "And second, what Church? All I give a damn about is that man and revenge, not some Church."

"The Church of Sinfinite Opportunity," I say. I wait for recognition to appear in her eyes, but it doesn't.

We start walking again, and I try to come up with a way to explain the Church to her. How she hasn't heard about it, I have no clue, but since she's now one of their victims, she deserves to know.

"Wait," she says and stops walking again. "Isn't that the trafficking ring that took your sister, Trinity?"

Anger pushes to break free, but not at Sylvia. Never at her. I'm angry—no, I'm fucking pissed—that Trinity will forever be linked to that damn ring. As if taking the majority of her life from her wasn't bad enough, she has to endure the constant recognition because of it.

"Yeah," I finally respond, not bothering to hide my emotions.

Sylvia's eyes soften a little, as if recognizing the broken pieces of me. Then she rests her hand on my bicep, quieting the beast inside the slightest bit.

"I'm sorry, Trainwreck," she says softly and shakes her head as if those words aren't good enough. "I was only gone for a couple weeks. I can't imagine what it was like for her and your family going through it for years."

Memories flash before me, spinning through the years so I get glimpses of the worst moments of my life: the day Trinity was taken, the day she was declared dead, her funeral, my parents' death... I'm transported through it all until I reach the day Trinity returned.

I shake free of Sylvia and shove those images from my mind.

"Let's go," I command.

It's another few minutes until we reach the club house and walk around it to the back entrance. When I open the door, Sylvia peers down the concrete steps leading to the Nightmare Room.

"Don't just stand here," I bark.

I take the steps two at a time, not bothering to see if Sylvia is following. The breeze at my back tells me the door is still open and she hasn't moved. When I get to the hallway outside of the room, I see Charlie, Fender, Trinity and Greaser. They're all hyper-focused on the monitor, watching Bartholomew.

Trinity spots me first and comes to stand next to me.

"You okay?" she asks.

"Fine, why?"

"Because *I'm* not, so how could you be?"

I narrow my eyes at her. She's right, but I don't want to tell her that and make her worry. "Just because we're twins doesn't mean we feel the same things."

Trinity tilts her head. "Tyler, it has nothing to do with being twins, although there's something to be said for it and you know it. This brings up a lot of shit for both of us. I just figured it would be getting to you."

"Well, you're wrong."

"No, you're not."

I swivel my head to see Sylvia standing on my other side. How did I not hear her?

"Neither of you know what you're talking about," I grit out and move toward the others.

Looking at the monitor, I see Bartholomew and my muscles coil tight, almost to the point of pain. I welcome the feeling.

"Has he been standing there this whole time?" I ask, nodding toward the screen.

"In the middle of the room, just like that," Fender replies.

"Asshole acts as if he doesn't have a care in the world," Charlie adds.

"He should," Greaser states matter-of-factly. "He may not be dying today, but he's sure as shit gonna feel what his victims feel."

"No," I say. "He'll feel a fraction of it. There's nothing we can do to him that will make him feel exactly what they did."

"We sure as hell can try though."

I glance down at Sylvia, who has once again snuck up beside me without me noticing.

"Yeah," I agree. "We can try."

Charlie claps her hands together. "So, who wants to go first?"

Fender looks at each of us, and when no one responds, he makes the call. "Ladies first."

Sylvia, Charlie, and Trinity exchange glances. Trinity is the only one to acknowledge what Fender said.

"I'm gonna sit this one out," my twin says. "I had my time in there." She nods at the door of the Nightmare Room. "I wanted to get a look at him, but I'm not exactly up for another round."

Greaser wraps his arm around his wife and pulls her into his side. "You sure?"

Trinity nods. "I'm sure. I'm going to go check on Trenton and soak up some of his laughter. I could use it." She shifts her focus toward the other women. "Give him hell."

She kisses Greaser before walking away and up the steps that will lead her into the clubhouse. I watch her, wondering how much emotional baggage she still has. No doubt a lot. I make a mental note to talk to Greaser and make sure she's okay because, just like me, she won't always own up to what's going on in her head.

"Syl, do you want to go in alone or together?"

Sylvia stares at her sister for a long time, so long I start to worry. Her face almost appears as if she's catatonic, but I know there has to be something running through her mind, whether it's flashes of memory or stone-cold rage.

Unable to handle the silence, I turn and step in front of her so I can look her in the eye. Charlie starts to protest, with her hand on my arm, but Fender stops her.

"Give him a sec," he instructs. Charlie huffs but does back off.

"Sylvia, look at me," I say, resting my hands on her shoulders. "Please?"

She glances at the monitor, and her body starts to shake. Her reaction isn't visible, but I feel it. She slowly shifts her eyes to lock with mine. "I can't go in there."

"Syl, you hav—"

"Charlie..." Fender's tone holds a hint of warning.

"Don't 'Charlie' me," she snaps. "She's my sister, and I know what she needs. I know what's best for—"

Sylvia stiffens and breaks her stare to look at her sister. "No, you don't!" she yells. "You always think you know what's best, but you don't have a fucking clue!" The pain in Sylvia's expression breaks my heart, and I find myself wanting to make it disappear. "We're two different people, Char. We may share some of the same experiences, what with growing up together and all, but this?" She stabs a finger in the air toward the monitor. "This isn't one of them. You've gotta stop trying to take over my life. I'm a big girl and can handle myself."

Charlie's expression is hard, cold... hurt.

"Maybe we should go upstairs," Fender suggests, wrapping an arm around his wife's waist. "Let Sylvia do what she needs to do."

"No." Charlie shakes her head. "I want a piece of him."

"He's not yours to get a piece of!" Sylvia shouts.

"Whoa, what the fuck is going on?"

We all turn toward the stairwell that leads to the clubhouse. Donovan is standing at the bottom, arms crossed over his chest.

"You're not supposed to be here," Fender snarls.

"Yeah, well, too fucking bad," Donovan counters. "Charlie may be more Soulless King than Black Savage, but Sylvia is still one of us. I told you from the beginning that I would be involved."

"Fine. But I'm telling you now," Fender begins. "What happens here stays here. Got me?"

Donovan nods as he moves closer to Sylvia. When he wraps his arms around her in a hug, a foreign emotion smacks me in the face. I can't readily identify it, but it deepens as she throws her arms around his neck. Whatever it is, I don't like it.

The hug goes on for what feels like forever, and I can't stand it. "Okay, time to break it up. This isn't the place for PDAs."

Fender's eyes snap to mine, and a grin tugs at his lips. It disappears so quickly, I tell myself I imagined it. I have to because there's nothing about this situation that's happy or funny.

Sylvia looks from Donovan to me and back again. "I'm glad you're here," she tells him. "I'm sorry I didn't listen to you at the party."

"Don't," Donovan says, his expression serious. "You have nothing to be sorry for. It's not your fault he's a monster."

"No, I know that. But—"

"Stop!" I grab her arm and whirl her around to face me. "He's right, this isn't your fault."

When it hits me that her eyes are wide and somewhat panicky, I remove my hand and thrust it through my hair. "Look, we can't go back and change what happened. All we can do is take care of business and move forward." I glance at the monitor then back to her. "So, do you want to take care of business?"

Sylvia stares at me for a second before nodding.

"Open the door."

Chapter Nine

His heart will still beat but that's about it.

Sylvia

Trainwreck presses a button on the wall, and the door to the Nightmare Room swings open. Before I know it, I'm face to face with Bob... no, Bartholomew. The lights flicker on, and I glance over my shoulder to see Trainwreck intensely watching me and giving me a thumbs up. Then the door closes and I'm alone with my captor.

Bartholomew looks me up and down, a sneer on his face. "I'd much prefer a dress." He nods toward my sweats. "This... *relaxed* look does nothing for you."

I glance down at my clothes before returning my attention to him. Ignoring his comment, I ask, "Why did you take me?"

"I didn't take you," he says. "I *acquired* you. *Bought and paid* for you."

"Whatever," I snap, annoyed that he didn't answer my question. "Why?"

He shrugs. "Why not?"

I take a step closer to him, fueled by his cavalier attitude, but freeze. The smirk on his face, his disgusting perusal of my body, taunts me, catapults me back to when he was in charge. My lungs seize and my knees threaten to buckle.

Bartholomew takes advantage of my hesitant state. "Ah, just as I figured. Not as brave as you thought, are you?"

I don't move. I *can't* move. My brain shouts at my limbs to do *something*, but nothing happens. It's as if each cell of my body is disconnected, one not having any effect on any of the others.

"And to think, I thought I wanted your sister," Bartholomew continues. "Charlie would be clawing my eyes out by now, wouldn't she? She'd be doing all the things your mind wants you to do but you can't." He tsks and shakes his head. "I much prefer this over a ballbuster like her. Easier to control, you know?"

The door swinging open startles me out of my stupor, and I look behind me just in time to see Trainwreck appear and launch himself at Bartholomew.

"You sick son of a bitch," Trainwreck snarls as he wraps his hand around Bartholomew's throat and shoves him back against the wall.

Bartholomew stumbles and air whooshes from his mouth, but other than that, he doesn't react. Most people would be clawing at the hands trying to strangle him, but not Bartholomew. No, he won't let us see his weakness.

You'll have fun trying to pull it out of him, though.

With that thought in mind, I rush toward the two men and latch onto Trainwreck's forearm.

"Trainwreck, stop!" I yell as I try to pull him off Bartholomew. "You have to let him go."

Trainwreck's eyes dart between his prey and me several times before he lowers his arm.

Bartholomew rolls his neck and grins.

"Wow, never thought I'd see the day when a big bad biker was bowing to the demands of a girl."

"Watch yourself," Trainwreck says as he leans in toward Bartholomew's face. "Wouldn't want me to forget that I'm supposed to keep you alive, now would we?"

"Alive, huh?" Bartholomew counters. "Interesting."

"It's really not." I'm annoyed that the two men are having a conversation as if they're the only two in the room.

I grab Trainwreck's hand and drag him toward the door. Surprisingly, he lets me, which I'm grateful for. I'm not sure I could have made him budge if he didn't want to.

"What are you doing?" I ask in a harsh whisper.

He narrows his eyes at me. "What do you mean?"

"Why did you come in?"

"Because he's a fucking asshole and needed put in his place," he says, so calmly I whole-heartedly believe he has no clue he just insulted me.

"I froze for a second." I shrug. "But I was fine. I can handle him, or 'put him in his place' as you say."

"I never said you couldn't handle him, Sylvia." Trainwreck reaches out and brushes my arm. "But I'm not sorry for stepping in and doing what I thought was necessary. I'm also not going to apologize for being here for you. Maybe in your club, standing back and watching a woman get treated like dirt is okay, but as a Soulless King, it's never okay. I'll never just stand idly by and let a man, or anyone, talk to you like that, *look* at you like that." He takes a deep breath and shoves a hand through his long hair. "I *am* sorry if I upset you though. That wasn't my intention."

I take in his words, but all I feel is confusion. Is Trainwreck acting this way because he's a Soulless King, or is he acting this way because it's me? I wish the answer to that question didn't matter. Hell, I never would have guessed it could matter, but it does... a lot.

"I can handle it from here," I tell him, hoping he believes it.

It's the truth, but even *I* can't completely dismiss the fact that I *did* hesitate. That's on me though, not Trainwreck. And until I can figure out why he's acting the way he is, or why I like it, keeping some distance will be good, for both of us.

"I know you can," he confirms as he pulls his phone out of his pocket and taps the screen. The door swings open again. "But you're not alone."

When Trainwreck leaves, all I can think is that maybe I *should* be. I've felt alone my entire life. Sure, I've had the club surrounding me, my parents and Charlie, but there's always been a part of me that felt like I was on an island by myself.

That was a lifetime ago... before you were kidnapped.

"Your boyfriend is a bit egotistical, isn't he?"

I turn back toward Bartholomew and quirk a brow. "First of all, he's not my boyfriend." I stalk toward him. "Second, Trainwreck is a good guy, so if you think you're gonna talk about him like you talked about me, think again. His reaction will make him seem like a kitten compared to mine."

"There's the lippy part of you I hate so much."

I swing my leg up, and the toe of my shoe connects with

Bartholomew's balls. He lets out a howl and bends to cup himself, as if that will alleviate the pain. He can act like a tough guy all he wants, but the second his balls are part of the equation, the facade crashes.

"What was that for?" he asks when he recovers and rises to his full height.

"Just because."

His face hardens, and his cheeks turn an angry red a split second before his hands grip my biceps and squeeze.

"Why did you do that?"

He shakes me like I'm a rag doll. I'll likely have bruises from his grasp, but I don't care.

Just like him earlier, I will not show my pain. But I will throw his own words back in his face.

"Why not?" I counter.

I spit on him, and he lets go of me so quickly, I almost topple over. Bartholomew scrubs so hard at the saliva on his face, one would think he had acid thrown on him.

When he deems himself clean, or as clean as he can be, his arms fall to his sides, and he clenches his hands into fists.

"That was uncalled for," he snarls. "And very unladylike."

"You say that like I'm supposed to care, like I should be ashamed of my actions."

His eyes widen. "You should—"

Blood spurts from his nose after I deliver a right jab to his face. Pain radiates through my hand, but I shake it off. There's no time for my pain, only his. That thought in mind, I punch Bartholomew, again and again and again, over and over until his face is a bloody mess. When I stop, he curls his lip.

"Is that all you got?" he asks, his teeth coated in crimson.

"You want more?"

I turn in a circle to really take in the Nightmare Room and see what I have to work with. Not much. I'm surrounded by concrete, some stained from previous occupants and some clean as can be.

"What do you need?"

I whip my head in the direction of the closed door when I hear Trainwreck's voice. Inspecting the room again, I see the speakers in the corners.

"What else ya got?" I ask him.

A loud noise catches my attention, and I tilt my head back to stare at the ceiling. It opens up and two sets of chains drop down.

"We've got it all," Trainwreck replies with a chuckle.

Impressed, I walk to the chains and pull on them to test their strength. I look at Bartholomew out of the corner of my eye, and that's when I see it... the tiniest hint of fear, like he's finally figured out that he's not walking out of this room. His heart will still beat, but that's about it.

I close the distance between Bartholomew and me, stopping when I can reach out and touch him. Part of me wishes he would fight for his life, but he won't. He thinks he's too refined for that. I twist his shirt in my fingers and drag him to the closest set of chains. He tries to resist, so I kick the back of his knee, causing it to buckle and him to fall.

I bend over him. "You're in my house now," I tell him. "Resist again, and I'll forget I'm not supposed to kill you."

Bartholomew's eyes light up as if I've divulged a deeply hidden secret.

"Don't get your hopes up, *Bob*."

I tug him the rest of the way to the chains and order him to get up. He doesn't resist, but he doesn't exactly make it easy for me to hang him by his wrists.

When he's secure, I grin at him.

"By the time I get done with you, you'll wish you were dead."

Chapter Ten

Stop the heart from beating, and the rest will follow.

Trainwreck

My eyes remain riveted on the monitor. Sylvia has been in the Nightmare Room with Bartholomew for over an hour now, and I can't stop watching. Several feelings have breezed through my mind: awe, pride, surprise... lust.

Sylvia has worn Bartholomew down, beaten him to within an inch of his life. It's a beautiful sight seeing a woman take out every last drop of pent-up anger on a man who tried to break her. I focus on Sylvia's face, and for the first time since carrying her out of that cage, she looks happy.

My phone vibrates against my leg, and I pull it out of my pocket. A text notification pops up, and I swipe the screen to open the full message.

Fender: How's she doing?

I watch as Sylvia uses the knife I gave her about twenty minutes ago to slash at the bottom of Bartholomew's feet while yelling about cold concrete floors.

Me: Great.

Fender: Is she getting information?

Me: Not yet.

Fender: Make it happen.

Me: Got it, Prez.

I push the lock button on the side of the cell and shove it into my pocket. Refocusing on Sylvia, I grin at the way she's carefully carving into Bartholomew's back. She's not cutting so deep that it'll kill him, but deep enough to make him beg her to stop.

Unfortunately, Fender's right. We need info, and we need it now… or at least soon if we want any chance of sticking to the plan. With that in mind, I press the intercom button.

"Sylvia, I hate to break this up…"

"So don't."

I sigh, hating myself for ruining her fun. "I don't have a choice."

She tosses the knife to the floor and looks up into what she assumes is a camera. It's not, but her message is clear… She's pissed.

"There's always a choice, Trainwreck," she snaps. "Always."

"Fine, then I choose to listen to my president. We need to start focusing on getting info outta this prick."

Sylvia runs a blood-soaked hand through her hair, leaving red streaks throughout the blonde. And when she wraps her hand around the back of her neck, I can't stop the thought that she's going to need a shower when we're done. And that turns into thoughts of her naked.

"Are you coming in or not?" Sylvia demands, her voice cutting through the haze my thoughts caused.

I have no idea how many times she's asked me that, lost in my fantasies the way I was, so I press the button to open the door to the Nightmare Room and it swings open.

"'Bout time," she grumbles as the door closes behind me.

"Sorry. I was, uh… texting Fender," I lie.

"Don't care," Sylvia says, heat in her tone. "Get the info you need and then give me five more minutes with him."

"Lippy, isn't she?" Bartholomew groans from his hanging position.

I lock eyes with Sylvia and grin. "I don't mind."

She darts her eyes away from me, as if embarrassed, and I wish there weren't blood spatter on her cheeks because I want to see her blush.

"Interesting." Bartholomew tries to lift his head to look at Sylvia. "I didn't think she was capable of embarrassment. She sure didn't display any when I had her."

I lunge at him in an effort to take him to the ground, completely forgetting about the chains. I hear a snap and almost instantly, Bartholomew screams in pain. I see a bone in his wrist poking through his skin, and a wave of satisfaction rolls through me.

Grabbing him by the hair, I yank his head back and get in his face.

"In case you haven't figured it out yet, you're not running this show," I snarl. "We are."

"That's where you're wrong." Bartholomew lets out a hollow laugh.

"What's so funny?" Sylvia asks, returning to the moment.

"You don't get it, do you?"

"Get what?"

"None of us are running this show."

"Then who?"

I look around the room at the faces of my brothers, of Black Savages, and am struck by the amount of respect surrounding me. Both clubs are meeting together to find out what Sylvia and I got out of Bartholomew, as well as see if we can move our plan forward with what we have.

"I don't know," I say to Donovan. "All he said was Lord Luxuria."

"Unfortunately, we only know of Conrad Templeton as Lord Luxuria, and he's dead," Squirrel adds. "We've been trying to figure out who's taken his place but have come up empty."

"I don't see how we can do anything without a name." Donovan's frustration is palpable.

"Maybe that's true, but we're not going to stop trying. We have to stop the Church of Sinfinite Opportunity. They can't keep taking people, children, from their families and off the streets to sell them. The cops can only do so much. We're the victim's—past, present, and future—only hope."

"It's an impossible task, Prez," Brick, a Black Savage,

adds. "They don't have anything, they didn't get anything, and we're wasting our time here."

"Sit the fuck down," Fender grits out.

Brick glares at Fender for a moment before Donovan intervenes.

"You heard him, Brick."

"Prez, are you real—"

"Sit. Down!"

Brick drops into the empty chair in front of him. If it weren't for his cut, all the tattoos, and the fact that I know he's hardcore when it comes to doing work for his club, I'd think he was a twelve-year-old in a snit because he isn't getting his way. He's fucking pouting and it's pathetic.

"You've seen the room full of information," Fender states, referring to my bedroom. He points to me. "If he can track down and eliminate everyone he did on his own, imagine what we can do together and with Bartholomew Jones at our disposal."

"Do we really have him at our disposal?" Brick counters. "He's hardly in any condition to help."

"He'll be fine," I bark. I turn to look at Gibson. "Right, doc?"

"I'll keep him alive," Gibson says slowly. His lips lift into a grin. "I'm just not sure how 'fine' he'll be. I don't know which one of you did the knife work, but it was good."

"That was all Sylvia," I respond, unable to stop a smile.

"Doesn't surprise me," Donovan says. "She's always had a thing for knives."

"You let her use a knife on him?" Brick accuses.

"Of course," I snort. "She asked for one. I sure as hell wasn't going to say no."

"Idiot."

"Watch it," Donovan warns Brick and the two of them exchange a look.

"Is there something we should know?" Fender asks. "And before you answer, remember, we're her family too."

"It's nothing," Donovan says. "It happened about two years ago, and we handled it."

Fender grabs Donovan by his cut and hauls him off his feet. "I swear to fuck, if you don't tell me what happened in the next ten seconds, we'll take out your entire club down the way we did your predecessor."

Donovan shrugs out of Fender's hold and brushes his hands down his torso. His face is set in stone, his shoulders stiff. The room is silent, tense, almost as if we're both waiting for them to kill each other.

Finally, Donovan heaves a sigh. "Sylvia has always been a bit wild." He chuckles humorlessly. "She and Charlie both were, but Sylvia would often take things too far."

"And two years ago?"

"Two years ago Sylvia went out, got blackout drunk, and went home with a guy she didn't know. When she woke up in the morning, she didn't recognize where she was or remember that she chose to go home with him. She reacted."

"Reacted how?" Fender asks with suspicion.

"She grabbed the knife she always carried and stabbed him. Many times." Donovan thrusts a hand through his hair. "She practically eviscerated the guy and then called me. Fortunately, it wasn't far away. I got there, paid off the roommate so the cops wouldn't be called, and got some of my prospects to go clean up the scene."

"And you never thought to call me, or her sister?"

"No, I didn't," Donovan snaps. "Sylvia isn't your problem. She's ours."

Unable to contain my frustration, I lunge from my chair and brace my hands on the table. "Sylvia is a fucking person, not a problem!"

"T, sit," Fender orders and returns his attention to Donovan. "We'll discuss this later. For now, we don't have time."

"No kidding," Piston speaks up. "We need to figure out what we're doing here, not argue about who belongs to who."

Squirrel types something on his laptop, and the information is mirrored on the big screen. "We might not have a name, but we have a location." He rises from his chair and walks to the screen to point at a red blinking dot. "Right here. This is the location of the main compound, just outside of Lodge Corner, Arkansas."

"That's gotta be what," Joker begins. "A thirty plus hour drive?"

"Depending on the route, thirty-one to thirty-six."

Fender focuses on me. "Trainwreck, you're in charge of things. What are you thinking?"

"I say we take out the compound," I answer without giving it a second thought. "We break the trip up over three days and spend our time off the road trying to figure out everything we can about who is still on my board. We take out the church, once and for all."

"You do realize that getting rid of the compound won't stop the die-hard followers, right?" Brick asks.

"Maybe not," I agree.

I walk to stand next to Squirrel and point to the same red dot.

"But stop the heart from beating, and the rest will follow."

Chapter Eleven

I forget that he knows my deepest, darkest secret.

Sylvia

I lift a forkful of medium rare steak to my lips and continue listening to Fender and Charlie talk about their day. After church, they both went to Infinite Motors to finish up a Harley that's to be picked up tomorrow by a customer. And if the mess Charlie's hair was in was any indication, they did a bit more than work.

Jealousy curls in my gut, and the bite of steak only aggravates it. What I wouldn't give to have what they have. Hell, what I wouldn't give to have someone in my life who cares about me even a little... and not because I'm family or was born into a certain club.

Trainwreck cares about you.

"Sylvia," Charlie snaps to get my attention. "Are you even listening?"

I shrug with another forkful of food halfway to my mouth. "Not really."

Charlie heaves a sigh and Fender speaks up. "I was just telling you both that Trainwreck has agreed to let you ride with him on the way to Arkansas."

"That's not gonna happen," I say matter-of-factly. "I'm riding my own bike."

Fender and Charlie exchange a glance that tells me World War III is about to start.

"Before you go and shit on my decision," I begin. "Remember, it's *my* decision. I'm not that girl, the one who needs a man around to take care of her or to make sure she gets from point A to point B. I'm perfectly capable of riding my own bike."

I set my fork down and lean back against the chair with my arms crossed over my chest, silently daring them to argue. Apparently, they like a good dare.

"Be reasonable, Syl—"

I lean forward and slap my hands on the table. "Be reasonable?!" I stand and shove my chair back so fast it almost topples over. "Reasonable, Charlie? Please, tell me how I'm not being reasonable. Because from where I'm standing, I'd say you two are the ones who aren't being reasonable."

"Sylvia, sit down." Fender points to the chair.

"Are you kidding me?" I half-heartedly chuckle. "In case you've forgotten, I'm not your ol' lady, and I'm sure as shit not a part of your club. You don't get to tell me what to do."

"Sit. Down." Fender enunciates the words and stares at me with cold eyes.

I throw my hands up and stomp away from the table toward the front door. "Fuck this!" I shout when I yank the door open and step out into the cold.

For a brief moment, I wish I'd grabbed the leather jacket

that was in the bag of clothes Brick brought me from home. Rather than go back inside, I wrap my arms around myself and start walking. Where I'm going, I have no clue.

I walk for what feels like hours, and my limbs shake from the cold. My teeth are chattering and yet, I keep walking. My destination doesn't matter. I wanted to get away from Fender and Charlie and I am.

I'd fully expected to see some of the other Soulless Kings out and about, especially since this is their property, but then again, it's dinner time. A lot of them have families, or significant others. Shit, all of them have bottomless pits for stomachs so it makes sense that they'd be home shoveling food into their bodies.

The sound of a motorcycle penetrates my thoughts, and I lift my head to see Trainwreck sitting on his Harley in front of his place. How the fuck did I end up here?

"Hey, Sylvia," Trainwreck calls to me. "What are you doing out here? It's freezing."

I tuck a strand of hair behind my ear before answering. "I could ask you the same thing."

"I was just heading to Chuggies to grab a drink," he replies. "Wanna come?"

I do, but I also don't want to admit it. And I definitely don't want to get on the back of his bike. It seems a pretty hypocritical thing to do after arguing about that very thing not that long ago.

"Nah, I'm good."

My voice quivers due to the cold. Truth be told, it's not all because of the weather. It's also a response to my complete lack of understanding why I ended up here and why I want to stay here, with Trainwreck... alone. It's frustration and confusion and excitement all rolled into one.

Trainwreck's eyes travel the length of my body, taking

in my hoodie with the Black Savages' logo, my tight jeans, and boots. When his gaze returns to my face, he's sporting a grin.

"Wanna go inside?" He hitches a thumb over his shoulder toward his house. "Have a drink or something?"

"Yes." I press my lips together. "I mean no." I shake my head at myself. "I mean, I don't want to ruin your plans."

Get it together, Syl. You've spent plenty of time with guys before, and Trainwreck is no different.

But he is different, and that's the problem.

"Which is it?"

"Which is what?"

"Well, you aren't ruining my plans. I've got plenty of alcohol inside," he says. "So is it 'yes' or 'no'?"

I pretend to think about it for a moment, as if I don't already know the answer. And I suppose there's a part of me that doesn't. But it's being overruled by the smaller part of me that knows exactly what I want to say.

Take me inside. Show me what it's like to be cared about. Prove to me that not all guys are bad, that not all of them care about one thing and one thing only.

I say none of that though.

"Yeah," I say with a nod. "I'll come in and have a drink." I close the distance between us as he cuts the engine of his Harley and gets off it. "But I can't stay long."

Trainwreck grins. "Okay."

He turns and walks to the door, pausing only to unlock it, and steps across the threshold. I follow him and watch as he tosses his keys and wallet on a table just inside the door and then saunters further in toward the kitchen.

Trainwreck takes several liquor bottles from a cabinet and sets them on the kitchen table.

"Pick your poison," he says.

He opens another cabinet and grabs two shot glasses before opening the refrigerator and pulling out two beers.

I scan the bottles, and my eyes light up when I see my favorite brand of whiskey. I point to it and say, "I'll have that."

"Nice choice." He pours us both a shot. "It's my favorite."

"Me too."

Trainwreck hands me my shot glass, clinks his with mine, and we both down our shots. I thrust my empty glass at him.

"Another."

He eyes me skeptically. "You sure?"

"C'mon, pour me another."

He does, and I savor the liquid as it travels a path toward my stomach.

"Make yourself comfortable." Trainwreck nods toward the couch behind me, which is pulled out into a bed. "I'll bring our beers in."

I stare at the furniture, not sure exactly where to sit. I don't want to give Trainwreck any ideas, so sitting on the pull-out couch isn't happening. But the chair is blocked and doesn't look comfortable with all his clothes strewn over it.

"Oh," he mumbles when he steps up next to me. "Sorry 'bout that."

He holds the beers out to me, leaving me no choice but to take them, and then he makes quick work of folding the bed. Next, he picks up his clothes and carries them down the hall to toss them in a room.

"Why are you sleeping on your couch?" I ask when he returns and takes one of the beers.

"Because I work in my bedroom."

"To take down the Church of Sinfinite Opportunity?"

He nods. "I started tracking their members on my own and there's so much information in there that it's easier to bring the brothers here than it is to take it all down and take it to the clubhouse."

"Makes sense."

I want to see everything he has, but I don't ask. Not yet. I don't know if my hesitation is because I'm not sure I really want to see it all or if it's because I'm afraid of the answer. If he says I can't see it, I know it'll upset me.

"I can show it to you if you want," he says as if reading my mind.

I take a pull from my bottle. "Maybe later."

"Okay."

We both sit on the couch, him on one end and me on the other. So close, yet so far away. I drink my beer in silence, and he does the same. It's awkward and confusing... and there's nowhere else I'd rather be.

Finally, I can't take it and speak. "So, Chuggies? Why not just go to the clubhouse?"

Trainwreck shrugs. "Wasn't in the mood for the clubhouse."

"Why not?"

"Just needed a change of scenery, I guess."

"Yet here we sit," I remind him. "Not exactly a change."

"Oh, this is a change."

I tilt my head. "How so?"

"Because you're here." Trainwreck scoots a little closer.

He's close enough to touch, and my stomach flip-flops. I tell myself it's the alcohol and not the man. It can't be the man. Despite that conviction, I make no effort to move.

"Why were you out walking?" he asks, and just like

that, my anger at Fender and Charlie comes rushing back, as does the reason I fled from their house.

"I needed some air," I say hotly, directing my anger at him.

"Whoa. Did I do something?"

"As a matter of fact, yes."

I stand from the couch and carry my beer to the trash. When I drop it in, it clanks against other empty bottles and fuels my anger. Something about the sound reminds me of fury, and I soak it up like a beach bum working on their tan.

"Okay," he says, dragging the word out. "Care to fill me in?"

I begin pacing, trying to come up with the right words. Normally, I wouldn't give a shit how I sound when I'm flipping out on someone. I'd just yell and get it out of my system. But right now, with Trainwreck, I don't want to do that.

I stop pacing in front of the couch and lock eyes with him. "Can I ask you something?"

"You can ask me anything."

Crossing my arms over my chest, I begin to tap my foot, needing to expel energy somehow.

"Why did you offer to let me ride with you to Arkansas?"

Trainwreck shoots up from the couch and closes the distance between us, his own anger flaring.

"Seriously?" he asks incredulously. "*That* is what this is about?"

I nod sharply and he narrows his eyes.

"Because it's the right thing to do," he says with conviction. "Because it's a long fucking ride, even split over three days, and that's hard on anyone. Because we're going to take out one of the evilest cults there is, and who knows what will happen on our way. Because..." He pauses and takes a deep breath before expelling it. "Just because."

What he says makes sense, and they're all good reasons, yet...

"But I'm not your ol' lady, or even your girlfriend." I shake my head in disbelief. "I'm just some chick you rescued from a psycho."

"Why does this bother you so much?" he counters. "Can't I just be a guy who's trying to do something nice for you?"

"No!" I shout. "Nice guys don't exist. Horny guys do, stupid guys, assholes, pricks, only-want-one-thing guys." I shake my head. "But nice guys? I have yet to meet one."

"Jesus, you have a warped view of the world."

"And how do you not with everything you've seen or with what happened to Trinity?"

Oh trust me, I do," Trainwreck tells me. "But I don't let it stop me from living." He takes a step closer to me. "If my offer pisses you off this much, I rescind it."

My stomach bottoms out. Huh. I thought that's what I wanted, but now that he's said the words, I realize it isn't even remotely close.

"Sylvia, I told you before, I'm always going to do what I think is right. And again, I'm sorry if I upset you, but I can't help who I am."

My face falls, and heat creeps into my cheeks. I rub my temples, trying to rid myself of a forming migraine.

"Shit," I mumble and stare at the floor. "I'm sorry. I didn't mean to go off on you. Bad habit I guess."

"Sylvia, look at me."

I try to look at him but can't bring myself to do it. Trainwreck lifts my chin with two fingers. My eyes dart away, trying to focus on anything other than him.

"Sylvia." His tone holds a hint of warning, or maybe it's promise. "Please look at me."

Finally, my eyes land on his face and he smiles.

"Is it so hard to believe I'm nice?" he asks as he shifts his hand from my chin to cup my cheek.

I nod, my mouth suddenly filled with cotton.

"I suppose you're right, to a degree," Trainwreck admits. "I'm not your typical nice guy. I do bad things and enjoy every second of it. I have a dark side." He nods toward his bedroom. "An obsessive side. I can't rest until my target is taken down." He rubs his thumb over my cheek, and I lean into his touch. "But I would *never* treat you like anything but the amazing woman you are. I am *nothing* but a nice guy where you're concerned."

I pull away from him to avoid leaning closer. "You don't even know me."

Trainwreck drops his arm and shoves his hands in his pockets. "I know you're sexy as hell regardless of if you're in sweats, a fancy dress, or jeans and a hoodie. I know you're smart and strong and more than capable of taking care of yourself. I know you don't let much get you down. You've got this quality that some might call bitchy, but not me. It reminds me that you have a backbone and don't need me. Which is good because if I'm ever going to take a chance on a chick, she's gotta be able to stand on her own two feet. I don't want someone who is only with me because she needs me. I want her to be with me because she wants me."

He takes one step forward, then another and another, until my back hits the wall from retreating.

"I know you killed a guy two years ago, and that doesn't change my opinion of you."

I open my mouth to protest just as he presses his body to

mine. Nothing but a moan escapes past my lips, an invitation.

Trainwreck leans close, pressing his lips to mine, and that's when I forget that he knows my deepest, darkest secret.

Chapter Twelve

Asking can make all the difference.

Trainwreck

Sylvia's lips are warm, silky, inviting. In the back of my mind, the fear is there that she'll pull away at any moment, and I try to ignore it. Right now, she's enjoying this as much as I am, if her moans and the way her body moves against mine are any indication.

I lift her up and press her into the wall, and she wraps her legs around my waist. Her hands thread through my hair as she tries to pull me closer. My tongue is practically down her throat so I'm not sure how much closer I can get.

I move my hands from beside her head and run them down her sides until I hit the top of her jeans. Just as she moans, again, my cell phone vibrates against my thigh causing me to groan and pull away, setting her on her feet.

Sylvia looks at me with questions dancing in her eyes. "Why are you stopping?"

I reach into my pocket and pull out my cell. "This."

Fender's name is across the top of the screen, and I can't stop another groan. I flip it around so Sylvia can see. "Him."

"Hello."

"Don't answer that."

Sylvia and I speak simultaneously, and she glares at me as if I didn't listen. Hard to listen when I've already done the thing she's telling me not to do.

"Have you heard from Sylvia?" There's worry in Fender's voice, which is unusual.

A quick glance at the woman I was just kissing, and I see her waving her hands. Clearly, she doesn't want Fender, or her sister, to know where she is. I mouth the words 'trust me' to her, and she throws her hands in the air before walking into the kitchen and yanking open the refrigerator door.

"Yeah, she's here, Prez," I respond. "Why, what's up?"

I put the phone on speaker so Sylvia can hear. My hope is that by doing so, she'll learn that she can trust me a little.

"Send her home," Fender demands.

Sylvia's head swings back and forth and she whispers, "I'm not going."

"Fender, you know as well as I do that I can't make Sylvia do anything she doesn't want to. She's your wife's sister, after all."

The second the words are out, I want to call them back.

"Are you refusing to obey an order?" he growls.

"No, not exactly." I push Sylvia's hand away when she tries to take the phone from me. "I'm merely pointing out that, even if I did tell her to leave and go straight to your house, it doesn't mean she'll listen."

"You could put her on the back of your bike and bring her here yourself."

"Holy shit," Sylvia lashes out. "You just don't get it, do you Fender? You're just like Charlie."

"What's that supposed to mean?"

"It means that both of you still see me as a little kid and not an adult. I've got news for you though. I grew the fuck up!"

"Maybe you should act like it then instead of running off when someone makes you mad. Face your problems, Syl, instead of pretending they don't exist."

"Fine, you want me to face my problem, Fender, let's face my problems. My entire life I've been invisible, always hidden in the shadow of my princess sister. I've fought against everything I was taught, ruined friendships, resisted relationships. I pretended that what happened to Charlie never happened to me."

She takes a deep breath, and Fender takes advantage of the pause.

"Are you saying Leal did things to you too?"

"Did you seriously think he didn't?" she snaps. "But I got through it and came out the other side stronger. I fixed myself. Sure, maybe I didn't do it the right way, but I did it my way, and it worked."

I listen to Sylvia's tirade with fascination, as well as a healthy dose of admiration, respect, and a little sadness. She's much stronger than I thought, than anyone has ever given her credit for. And she's every bit as close to perfect for me as I was starting to think.

"Oh..." She snaps her fingers. "And let's not forget that I was taken by a man I had no intentions of doing more with than fucking. I was held for almost two weeks, raped repeatedly, dressed up like a goddamn doll and treated like a possession. And yet, here I stand, still fucking breathing, still living, still taking care of myself." Her body deflates.

"So, please, Fender, don't for a second tell me I don't face my problems because I face them head on. It's everyone else who walks away and doesn't see them."

With that, Sylvia storms out the front door. The walls rattle when it slams shut behind her. I try to move, needing to go after her, but am frozen by my loyalty to Fender and the club.

"She just left, didn't she?" Charlie's voice comes through the line. Of course Fender would have the call on speaker. I sure did.

"That's the first thing out of your mouth after everything she just said?" I can't stop the question. My brain tried, screamed at me to hold it in, but I simply couldn't.

"Watch it," Fender warns.

"No disrespect, Prez, but I need to find Sylvia. Somebody needs to show her she's not alone."

I end the call knowing I'm going to pay for my words later. But I don't care. Sylvia's worth it.

On my way out, I snag my keys and wallet off the entry table. I yank open the door and come to a halt because there she is, sitting on my steps, her knees drawn up to her chest.

I cross the porch and lower myself next to her, remaining silent. We sit there for several minutes, both staring straight ahead, yet not at anything in particular.

"I'm sorry you had to hear all of that." Her voice is barely above a whisper, forcing me to lean in to hear her.

"You have nothing to be sorry for, Sylvia." I turn to face her and lean back against the railing. "Hey, do you remember the night we met?"

"It was a party, right?"

I nod. "Charlie brought you so you could meet everyone." I tilt my head back slightly, remembering. "It's been several years, but I still remember walking into the main room at the clubhouse. I saw you standing among a few of the brothers and whatever Bangin' Betties were hanging on to them."

"That feels like a lifetime ago."

I chuckle. "Uh huh. It might as well have been for all we've both been through." I wave my hand, dismissing that train of thought. "Anyway, I made a beeline for you like some green teenager, and you were having none of me. It didn't matter though. I had a crush on you the moment I laid eyes on you."

Sylvia twists to look me in the eye. "What are you saying, Trainwreck?"

"You can call me Tyler, ya know?"

"Tyler?"

"Yep. That's my real name."

"Yeah, yeah, I figured. But why would I call you Tyler?"

I shrug. "You don't have to. I guess I just want you to know that there's more to me than this club. I'm not just Trainwreck. I've done a lot of growing up since we met and lived a lifetime in those few years. I can't sit here and pretend that I spent these years pining for you because of some silly crush. That would be a lie. But it would also be a lie if I said that my crush hasn't come rushing back. It'd be a lie if I said I didn't want to see if there's something between us. It would be a lie if I said I don't want to know everything there is to know about you, good and bad."

"Well, you just heard quite a lot."

"I did," I confirm. "Yet here I am." I lift Sylvia's hand to thread my fingers through hers. "Nothing you said has made me want to run. In fact, all of it makes me like you even more."

Sylvia stares at me, emotions fluttering across her face: confusion, sadness, skepticism... hope.

"I've never done the whole relationship thing," she says.

"I'm not asking for a relationship," I assure her.

"Then what are you asking for?"

"A fucking chance. All I want is for you to be open to the possibility that I'm not like every other guy out there, or even like anyone else in your life right now. All I'm asking is for you to trust me a little. I'm asking you to ride with me to Arkansas."

At some point while I was talking, it hit me that sometimes people need to be asked instead of told what to do. *Asking* can make all the difference.

"I'm asking for a chance, Sylvia."

Chapter Thirteen

The moment I made up my mind to give him a chance, every cell of my being decided he could be trusted, that he was perfect for me in every way.

Sylvia
Three days later...

"You're seriously going to let someone else take your Harley?"

I shove the rest of my clothes into the duffel back on the bed in front of me before lifting my head to look at Charlie. She's standing in the doorway, leaning against the frame with her arms crossed over her chest.

"That's what I've said for the last few days. Still not listening to me, I see."

"Syl, that's not fair. You know how crazy it's been around here, what with trying to get ready for the trip to Arkansas and the guys planning the attack when we get there. I've hardly had time to process my own thoughts, let alone listen to yours."

"Good to know."

I zip the bag before slinging it over my shoulder and pushing past Charlie to leave the room. Charlie follows.

"Where are you going?"

"To the clubhouse. We leave in an hour."

"I know when we leave," she snaps. "But we're talking."

"No, Charlie, we're not. You're talking, or trying to at least, and I'm walking away." I open the front door and step out onto the porch, Charlie on my heels. I whirl around to face her. "I'm not in the mood to talk. Maybe later, or another day, but not now." I drop my bag and rest my hands on her shoulders. "You're my sister, and I love you, Charlie. But you've gotta give me space to figure things out on my own. Just give me time."

My sister's shoulders slump. "I just don't think..."

The sound of an approaching Harley pulls our attention away from each other, thank God. I don't know that I could have stood here a second longer while my sister tried to tell me what I'm doing wrong and how I should do it right.

Brick stops his bike at the bottom of the steps and grins at me, almost ignoring Charlie. "Need a ride, babe?"

Babe?

We may have had an on and off thing before, but that feels like a millennia ago. I remind myself that Brick is a ladies' man and talks to most women like that. I'm nothing special to him. We're just friends, and if he wants to call me 'babe', that's fine, as long as he doesn't cross that friendship line.

"Sure," I finally respond.

Brick gets off his bike and walks up the steps to grab my bag. He presses a kiss to Charlie's cheek.

"You look annoyed, Char. What's up?"

Charlie darts me a look before focusing on Brick. She

shakes her head. "Nothing. Just have a lot to do before we leave. If you'll excuse me..."

She disappears into the house, shutting the door behind her. The lock clicks into place.

"What's her deal?" Brick carries my bag to the bike.

I look over my shoulder at the door and stare for a moment, as if I'm looking through it at Charlie to find the answer.

You know the answer.

I turn and join Brick at the bottom of the steps. "No deal. She's just tired," I lie.

I may be fighting with my sister, but that doesn't mean I need to broadcast that to everyone. Especially Brick, who likes to run his mouth. The second he had a chance, he'd run to Donovan, who would go to Fender, and then it would turn into this whole big thing. This is between me and her, not the world.

"C'mon, let's get to the clubhouse."

Brick offers me his hand to help me onto the Harley. I roll my eyes and ignore it. He knows better than to do that. I've made it clear to him, over and over again, that I don't need his help to get on a motorcycle. I grew up on them.

He climbs on in front of me, and we take off toward the clubhouse. The ride is short, and I'm careful not to hold onto him more than I have to. He tries to rest his hand on my thigh, but I shake it off. There was a time I loved it when he touched me. That time has passed.

When we pull up in front of the clubhouse, there are no less than twenty-five bikers either engrossed in conversation or looking over their own bikes. The Soulless Kings' van is there, and I can't help but wonder if Bartholomew is already inside.

The plan to take out the Church of Sinfinite Opportunity is simple, but there are a lot of moving parts. Something tells me we'll all work together like a well-oiled machine, although that doesn't mean there aren't things outside of our control. Bartholomew isn't one of those things. Hence, the van.

The trip will take three days. Two brothers, whether Soulless King or Black Savage, will be in the van at all times with our prisoner. One will drive, and the other will keep working on Bartholomew for information, not that I think they'll get any. In my opinion, he should be dead. But I'm not in charge.

Every night we'll stop at a motel, and someone will take a shift staying in the van with Bartholomew. He will never be alone, nor will he ever be permitted outside of the van. It's safer that way. Trainwreck's shift is on night three. When we're about an hour from Lodge Corner, Arkansas, we won't go straight to the compound. No, we'll get some rest so we can attack in the wee hours of the following morning, before sunup.

And through all of it, I'll be on the back of Trainwreck's bike. I tried to explain this to Charlie, that I agreed to ride with him because he *asked*. And I also tried to tell her that I only agreed with a few stipulations. First, I get to pick who uses my Harley, and I chose Royal. Second, if I decide I want to drive alone, I can, and Royal can either ride bitch with someone or in the van. And third, just because I'm riding with him doesn't mean we'll share a room at the motels.

Although, I wouldn't exactly be opposed to it. I just don't want him to expect it. I'm in control of what goes down between us at night. The possibilities are endless. I shiver at the thought.

"You ready for this?"

Trainwreck's voice startles me from my thoughts. I was so deep in them that I didn't even notice that Brick's gone or hear Trainwreck walk up. Before I can look him in the eye, I get off the bike and bend to wipe my sweaty palms on my jeans. When I straighten, he's watching me intently.

I clear my throat. "Ready as I'll ever be."

And not just for the trip to Arkansas.

Trainwreck steps closer and wraps a hand around the back of my neck. He caresses my skin with his thumb, and heat swirls through my system to settle between my legs. He leans in and whispers, "Your cheeks are bright red, Syl. Why is that?"

His voice is a deep rumble, and I shiver again. He may not have seen the first shiver, but he sure as hell can feel this one.

"I, um... it's the wind," I stutter.

He pulls his head back to look me in the eyes, his brow quirked. "The wind?"

I nod. "From the ride here."

"The five-minute ride here, huh?"

"Yep."

Trainwreck chuckles. "Okay, whatever you say."

He releases me and gets my bag from Brick's bike before leading me to his own. He puts it with his, and I catch sight of the stash of weapons. When Trainwreck's done, he looks at me and then grabs a sheathed knife.

"Here." He hands me the blade.

I don't even hesitate. I snatch the knife from him and pull it from the sheath to hold it in front of me. I admire the craftsmanship, and when I flip the knife over, I see the engraving.

SYLVIA'S STABBING GRACE

"Wait." I search his eyes. They tell me nothing. "This is mine?"

"That's your name, isn't it?"

"Yes, but..." I shake my head to clear it. "When did you get this?"

"This morning," Trainwreck responds as he rocks back on his heels. His eyes are spilling all of his secrets now... he's nervous. "You like knives, right? I figured you didn't have one of your own since everyone seems determined to make decisions for you, so I got you one. It's nothing, really. Just a way to protect yourself."

I shove the knife back into its holder and launch myself into Trainwreck's arms. He catches me easily and holds me close.

"You like it?"

I laugh outright. "Are you kidding me? I love it."

Trainwreck's body relaxes, but not his embrace. "Good."

He sets me on my feet, and my body protests, silently begs him to hang on a little longer. It's almost as if the moment I made up my mind to give him a chance, every cell of my being decided he could be trusted, that he was perfect for me in every way.

I place my hand on his cheek. "Thank you, Tyler."

He grins. "For the knife?"

"Yeah, partly."

My lips lift into a smile.

"But mostly for being you, for actually being a nice guy."

Chapter Fourteen

She can't hurt me.

Trainwreck

One hour down.

Nine hours to go... today.

One hour of torturous contact. One hour of my insides being ignited by the feel of Sylvia against my back. One hour of fantasies racing through my mind and the logical part of my brain shutting them down.

One fucking hour and nine more to go.

Sylvia's hands rest on my hips, her fingertips sending electric shocks through my system every time they move. I want to wrap my hand around her leg but haven't been able to bring myself to do it yet. She trusts me, and I don't want to cross a line she's not ready to cross. And if she is ready, well, she needs to find a way to let me know.

While I can't bring myself to touch her leg, I can't stop looking down at it. As if reading my mind, Sylvia reaches around me, grabs my hand, and brings it to rest exactly where I wanted it.

"You can touch me, Tyler," she yells to be heard over the roar of all the Harley engines surrounding us.

I nod.

For the next two hours, I use my hand to explore her thigh. I drive myself crazy, and the feeling is only amplified by my wondering if I'm doing the same to her. I think I am because every once in a while, her fingers dig into my sides like she's trying to keep her reaction under control.

Fender leads the group off the interstate and toward a McDonald's where we can stretch our legs. Our caravan is so large, we fill the entire parking lot, some of us two or three bikes to a space. There were only four other vehicles when we arrived.

Both Sylvia and I get off my Harley. She lifts her arms above her head in a stretch, and her tits press against her hoodie, drawing my eyes to them. Her sweatshirt is form-fitting, and I want to yank it over her head.

"My eyes are up here," she says.

"I know." I make no move to look away from her chest.

Sylvia laughs and that does the trick. I could listen to her laugh for hours. I could stare at her for hours too, but that's beside the point. Any amount of time spent looking at or listening to Sylvia could never be enough.

"We've got thirty minutes," Fender calls out to everyone. "Make the most of it."

He disappears inside with Charlie on his arm. Most of the Soulless Kings follow him, and the Black Savages stay outside. We may be working together, but for now, we're separate.

"You hungry?" Sylvia asks me.

My mind wanders, and I peruse her from head to toe. "Very."

At that moment, Brick walks up to us and wraps his arm around Sylvia's waist. Rage rolls through me, and it takes every ounce of control I barely possess not to level him.

"Ready to eat, babe?"

Sylvia's eyes dart from mine to Brick's before she pulls herself free and spins to face him. "What are you doing?" she hisses.

Brick looks stunned for a moment but quickly recovers and holds his hands up in mock surrender. "Nothing."

"No, Brick, it's not *nothing*. You keep calling me 'babe' like you have a right to. In case you haven't noticed, I've moved on."

"Oh, I've noticed." His expression shifts to disgust. "You've been hanging all over him for the last three hours. He's lucky I haven't pummeled him for touching you."

"Are you fucking kidding me?" Sylvia hisses. "You have no right to get upset. We are not a thing." She waves her hand in the space between them. "We never really were."

Disgust morphs into a rage Brick can't disguise. "We've been fucking on and off for years," he snarls. "You can't just walk away from that, from me."

Unable to control myself any longer, I haul my arm back and deliver a blow to his face. Brick may be bigger than me, but I've got anger fueling my actions and that can make a man stronger than he appears.

I hit Brick again, and then again, before grabbing a hold of his shoulders and pulling him down so I can ram my knee into his stomach. When I do that, he falls to the ground with a groan.

I squat next to him and get in his face. I speak low so only he can hear what I say. "You may have been fucking her, but whose bike is she on the back of?" I grab him by the throat and use as much force as I can without taking his life. "If you ever talk to her like that again, I won't be so forgiving."

I stand up straight and step next to Sylvia. Her arm comes around my waist, and she squeezes.

"That was hot." She grins devilishly. "But I could have handled it."

"I know you could have. But I couldn't *not* handle it."

"I'm gonna have to get used to this, aren't I?"

"Fuck yes." I put my arm around her shoulders as I guide her inside. "If you're going to be with me, yeah, get used to it."

Sylvia dips her head for a moment before lifting it and locking eyes with me. "I think I can do that."

WE'VE BEEN BACK ON THE ROAD FOR SEVERAL HOURS and from the moment we pulled out of the parking lot, Brick has been on my tail. Maybe I picked the wrong time to let my anger get the best of me, but I couldn't stop it. I don't give a shit what club you're a part of, you don't mess with another man's woman.

Is she your woman, though?

We might not have put a label on what we are, but Sylvia is mine. She belongs to me. Not Bartholomew, not some random guy who tries to pick her up at a bar, and certainly not fucking Brick. Me.

While we ate, Sylvia filled me in on her history with Brick. And from the sound of it, there was never a relationship... not one that mattered anyway. I'd be lying if I said I wasn't a little jealous of any man who's been inside her, but at the end of the day, I'll be the last man to have that privilege and that means something.

The last man? Now you sound like you've found the one.

I'm not so sure about that, but I'm going to treat her like she is. Because that's what she deserves.

Sylvia shifts behind me, and I tighten my hold on her leg. She taps my side and points to the left. I turn my head in time to see Brick pulling out around us and speeding toward the front of the group. He flips me off as he passes, and my lips lift into a grin. He weaves in and out of the rest of the bikers until he's next to Donovan.

"Ignore him," Sylvia yells.

"I am."

That's not exactly true. I am in the way that she means. I'm not letting him get to me so far as his history with Sylvia is concerned. But I can't completely ignore him. He's got those bruises I created that are so much fun to look at. Not only that, but he's a hot head. I don't think everyone can see it, but I do. Because it's like looking in a mirror. There's something simmering under the surface with Brick, I just can't quite put a finger on what it is.

Another hour passes before we take another break, this time at a rest area off the interstate. We aren't there for more than twenty minutes, and when we get back on the road, Sylvia's arms come around my waist and she rests her cheek against my back.

For the rest of today's leg of the trip, I ride toward the front, close to Greaser. Trinity wanted to come, but she and Holland stayed back to take care of the kids. Luna and Riley are with us because of their skill sets. They could prove to be valuable in our attack. That being said, Joker and Riker aren't exactly thrilled that their ol' ladies were approved to come because it'll divide their attention. But Fender gave the okay, and what he says goes.

The sun falls below the horizon as we exit the interstate and find the motel we're staying at. Charlie made reservations for everyone. Unfortunately, we have to split up between three motels because apparently, barely-a-blip-on-the-map towns still get some people traveling through and needing a bed.

The group separates, each of us going to our designated resting place for the night. We pull into the parking lot, and I breathe a sigh of relief when I see that it's all Soulless Kings at our motel. I'm glad we have the Black Savages with us, but I'll sleep better knowing I'm only surrounded by my *own* brothers... and Sylvia. She has her own room, but there was no way Charlie was going to put her sister at a different location.

Charlie goes into the motel office to check us all in, Fender following close behind. She can handle herself, just like Sylvia, but Fender will always do his own thing in order to make sure she's safe.

"I don't know about the rest of you fuckers," Joker says when he steps up next to me. "But I'm ready for a break."

Joker has his arm around Riley's shoulders, and she looks up at him and winks. "I know I could."

"Why do I get the feeling you two aren't going to get much sleep?" Riker asks.

"Bro, we aren't going to be doing anything you two aren't." Joker moves his finger between Riker and Luna. "Don't pretend it isn't going to be a fuck fest in at least three of the rooms tonight." He glances at me. "Maybe four."

"That's enough," Fender barks when he and Charlie return to the group in the parking lot. "Here are everyone's keys." He begins passing them out.

"Where's mine?" Sylvia asks when he's done.

"You'll have to bunk with us," Charlie tells her. "They were a room short."

"I'm not sleeping in the same room as you two." Sylvia looks at me, and her eyes light up before she returns her attention to Charlie. "I'll stay with Trainwreck."

"I don't think—"

"I don't give a shit what you think, Char," Sylvia snaps.

"T, come with me," Fender orders and walks a few feet away.

I follow him but am still tuned into Sylvia and Charlie arguing.

"What's up, Prez?"

"Are you okay with her staying with you?"

Fuck yes, I'm okay with it!

"Of course, if that's what she wants."

Fender heaves a sigh and runs a hand through his hair. "I'm trying really hard not to boss her around. It's not easy, believe me. But Sylvia's right, she's not a child. And after everything she's been through? I don't know... I want to protect her, but I'm beginning to wonder if my wife isn't taking it a little too far."

"All due respect, she is." I glance over my shoulder at the sisters, who are no longer arguing. They *are* staring each other down though. "I think we've all learned, or should have at least, that we can't stop the bad in the world. We can do our part to clean it up a bit, but we can't stop it. Charlie can't save Sylvia. And not because she's not capable, but because Sylvia doesn't need saving. Hell, I'm not sure she needs protecting."

"That doesn't exactly inspire confidence that you'll keep her safe."

That hurts. After what my twin went through, how

could he possibly think I wouldn't do everything in my power to protect Sylvia?

"I can assure you, Sylvia is as safe as she can be with me."

Fender's face twists, and his eyes become hyper focused on mine, almost as if he's trying to assess something he can't see. "And what about you, T? Are you safe with *her*?"

The question shocks me. "You think she's going to stab me like she did that other guy?"

"Not what I meant."

My forehead scrunches as I try to figure out what he's trying to say. It hits me in a rush. Well, fuck.

"My heart is just fine, man," I assure him. "She can't hurt me."

"She's a woman, T. She can hurt anything with a cock."

Chapter Fifteen

He sure knows how to turn a girl on.

Sylvia

Lukewarm water trickles over me. The moment we stepped into the room, I told Trainwreck I needed a shower, and here I am. I just wish I'd have known how horrible the heat and water pressure was.

I glance around for the standard sample size shampoo and conditioner that are normally provided and see none. Dammit!

I whip the shower curtain aside and yell for Trainwreck.

"Yo," he says as he throws open the door just as I pull the curtain back into place.

I can't stop the laugh that bubbles up my throat. "Were you standing right outside the door?"

"No. This room is just that damn tiny."

"Right." I peek around the edge of the curtain. It's only an opaque liner so I know he can see a pretty decent outline of my naked body, but I'll keep pretending I have some modesty left. "Can you grab my shampoo and conditioner out of my bag? They don't have shit here."

"Sure thing." He disappears and returns a minute later with both bottles in hand. "Here."

I reach out to grab it, dripping water onto the floor as I do, and our fingers touch. Electricity zings through my hand, up my arm, and then down my torso straight to my clit. He might as well have touched me himself.

"Thank you."

His eyes travel almost the same path the electric shock did and closes the distance between us. "Need help in there?"

I consider his question. I don't need the help to take a shower, but we both know that's not what he was referring to. And as much as I want him in here with me, naked as I am, I'm not ready. I'm horny as hell, sure, but that's not enough. Not if I want to give whatever there is between us a real shot.

I smile to soften my response. "I'm good."

Trainwreck's face falls for a split second, but then he smiles. "Okay. I'm here if you need anything."

With that, he walks out of the bathroom, pulling the door shut behind him. I stare at the metal barrier, silently wishing I'd have asked him to stay.

No. No, no, no. You did the right thing.

I adjust the water temp to see if I can get it any hotter before washing my hair. Once that's done, I look for a bar of soap and thank God when I spot a tiny one. I unwrap it and lather my body.

My fingertips brush my nipples, and they harden at the touch. I move my hands lower, over my stomach, and cup my mound as I press my middle finger against my clit. My legs shake, and I brace myself against the retro, jade green tile that surrounds the tub.

Just because I said no to Trainwreck doesn't mean I can't take care of myself. As I circle my clit, I imagine Trainwreck is kneeling in front of me, his tongue in place of my finger. I alternate between circles and light flicks, ramping up my desire, the pictures in my mind getting dirtier, more erotic as I do.

"Mmm," I moan, doing my best to be quiet.

I lift my leg and rest my foot on the soap holder to allow easier access to my pussy. I shove two fingers inside myself and thrust in and out while my imagination goes wild. I envision grabbing Trainwreck's hair and pushing his head closer to my core, forcing his tongue deeper. He slaps his hands on my ass and pulls me toward him, his nose buried against my clit while he laps at my juices.

My legs threaten to buckle, but I manage to stay upright through the most intense solo orgasm I've ever had.

"Ahhhh... mmmm."

I remove my fingers and rub my clit until the pleasure turns to pain. Doubling over, I rest my hands on my knees, trying to catch my breath. Holy fucking hell. If just thinking about him does that to me, what would the real thing feel like?

Once I'm confident I can stand upright without crumbling into a satisfied heap in the tub, I wash myself off as if to remove any evidence of my masturbating. I turn the shower off and open the curtain before grabbing the rough, worn-out cotton towel off the toilet seat lid.

The towel is tiny, as expected in a cheap place like this, and I'm not even able to wrap it around my body. I dry off as best I can and then realize I didn't bring any clothes into the bathroom with me. Motherfucker!

I hold both ends of the towel as closely together as I can and open the door. Leaning against the wall just outside the bathroom is Trainwreck, arms crossed over his bare chest, legs crossed at the ankles. And he's wearing a giant grin.

"Was it good for you?" he asks.

"You heard that?" Heat licks up my skin. I don't know if it's from embarrassment or if I'm turned on by the fact that he heard.

"Hard to miss when you're yelling my name. I came to make sure you were okay." His grin widens. "Imagine my surprise when I heard you moaning."

I drop my head to stare at the floor. "I, um... shit."

He closes the distance between us and cups my cheeks, lifting my head as he does. "I liked it, Sylvia." He smirks. "A lot."

I search his eyes for any sign that he's teasing me, or worse, upset with me for getting off without him. What I find instead is desire, conviction, desperation... satisfaction. I glance down for confirmation of my thoughts. His jeans are undone and he's not wearing anything underneath them.

He's telling the truth. He *did* like it.

"And now that we're both more *relaxed*, I'm going to need you to put some clothes on. Otherwise, I'm not going to be able to stop myself from pushing for the real deal."

"Okay."

"I want you, Sylvia. I need you." Trainwreck moves his hands from my face and trails a fingertip down my neck to my collarbone, and then lower still until he reaches the top of the towel that's barely covering me. "But I can be a patient man when I have to be. And for you, I'll wait. Just don't make me wait too long."

A shiver races down my spine, both from his touch and his words. He sure knows how to turn a girl on.

Trainwreck steps aside so I can move past him and get dressed. I have no doubt that he was serious when he said he needed me to put clothes on. I need that too because he's right. There will be no control if I don't.

I dig through my bag for the shorts and T-shirt I brought to sleep in. The bathroom door closes, and I glance over my shoulder to see I'm alone. I quickly throw my clothes on, and a minute later, when Trainwreck steps out of the bathroom, I'm completely covered and stretched out on the bed.

He stops in his tracks and stares at me. Trainwreck studies me, trails his gaze over my face, my chest, my legs.

"What have I gotten myself into?" he mumbles.

Before I can answer, a knock on the door startles me. I sit up so fast my head spins while Trainwreck answers it. I can't see who's there, but I recognize the voice.

"I need to talk to Sylvia," Donovan says, his tone leaving no room for argument.

Trainwreck swings the door wide and Donovan steps inside. When he sees me on the bed, he narrows his eyes.

"What's going on here?" he demands.

I roll my eyes and stand up. "Nothing. Jesus, I was just trying to relax. It's been a long day."

Donovan gives a curt nod. "Yeah, it has." He rubs his forehead. "I need you to come outside for a minute, Syl."

"Why?"

"Because I need to talk to you."

"Okay, so talk."

Donovan glances at Trainwreck and then back at me. "Outside. Now."

Huffing out a breath, I yank the comforter off the bed and wrap it around myself. It's fucking cold outside. I follow

Donovan out the door and across the parking lot to where his bike is parked.

We both stop and he turns to face me. My teeth begin to chatter from the cold, and I pull the blanket tighter.

"Care to explain what happened today?" Donovan crosses his arms over his chest and stands with his feet braced apart. He's angry. "I've gotten Brick's side of the story and now I need yours."

"Seriously?" I heave a sigh. "It was nothing. Brick was being an asshole, and Trainwreck put him in his place."

Donovan glances over his shoulder at the motel room, and I follow his gaze. Trainwreck is standing at the window, the flimsy curtain pulled to the side, and he's watching us. While that would normally bother me, I find I don't mind it so much with Trainwreck. He doesn't do it due to a lack of trust or belief in my ability to take care of myself. He does it because he gives a shit about me.

"That's not what Brick says."

"And what does he say happened? Please, enlighten me, because it can't possibly be the truth if you're this upset about it."

"Look, I saw Brick wrap his arm around your waist. There was a time you'd have eaten that shit up. You and Brick have a history you can't ignore. He might not be perfect, but at least he's one of us."

"Careful, Donovan. You're starting to sound like you did the night I was taken."

"And I was right that night," he counters hotly. "I told you Pete was bad news, and you chose to ignore me. I'm doing the same thing now. Trainwreck is bad news, Syl. He's got a one-track mind when it comes to the Church of Sinfinite Opportunity, and you know it. He'll do whatever it takes to get to them, including use you."

"He's not using me," I argue. "If anyone was using me, it was Brick."

"I think that went both ways, Syl."

"Yeah, it did. Brick and I used each other," I admit. "But we were both consenting adults who knew what we were doing. Trainwreck isn't using me. He's different."

"No, Sylvia, he's not. You just don't want to see it."

Donovan straddles his bike but keeps his focus on me.

"Trainwreck got a free pass today, but only because I don't make a habit of getting involved dick measuring contests. If you're so determined to stick by him and turn your back on your family, fine. But keep your boy toy in check so I don't have to."

Chapter Sixteen

When I'm watching the life drain from their eyes, I feel euphoric.

Trainwreck

I know I shouldn't be watching Donovan and Sylvia in the parking lot, but I can't help myself. When he pulls out of the parking lot, I let the curtain fall and move to sit on the bed. I left the door propped open so Sylvia can get back in without her key.

She shoves the door open and slams it behind her. After she slides the chain lock into place, she crosses to the other bed and plops down.

"Everything okay?"

Sylvia glares at me. "Does it look like it?" She pulls the blanket from around her and stretches out. "I saw you watching. I'm pretty sure you can answer your own question."

"Fair enough."

She turns toward me to lay on her side, propping her

head on her hand. "Do I really come across as some flimsy chick who doesn't know shit about the world, about life?"

"Is that what he said?"

Sylvia rolls her eyes. "He might as well have."

I mirror her position. "No, you don't come across that way."

"Then why does everyone insist on acting like I do?"

"Because they care."

My answer comes out sounding like a question. I don't mean it to, but maybe it is. I can't speak for anyone but myself.

"They have a funny way of showing it."

"Maybe." I shrug. "Or maybe it's normal? I don't know..."

"But?" she asks.

"But I know what it's like to have someone you love be hurt in ways that are unfathomable. I know how it feels to want to fix something that can't necessarily be fixed."

"Trinity?"

I nod. "I was only nine when she was taken, and we're twins, so it's not like I was older and wiser or anything. But she's still my sister, and I always felt like she was mine to protect. Maybe not before the kidnapping, but certainly after. Still do, really. I grew up real fast after that."

"You were just a kid."

"Doesn't matter."

I roll to my back and stare at the ceiling. I don't like to talk about what happened to Trinity. It opens wounds I've slapped band aids on countless times in an effort to heal them. Talking about my pain only amplifies the rage, darkens my soul more than it already is. How much blacker can it get?

"We should get some sleep," I finally say. "We've got another long day tomorrow."

"You're avoiding the subject," she accuses.

"Yeah, I am. It's not one I like to revisit."

"Is it really revisiting it, though? When you're still living every day trying to take down the organization responsible?"

I glare at her. "How did this get turned around on me? We were talking about you."

"You're the one who asked for a chance, Tyler," she reminds me. "I'm giving you that, giving *us* that. But it'll only work if we're both open and honest with each other."

"That goes both ways."

"I'm aware of that."

"Then tell me what happened two years ago." I sit up and swing my legs over the edge of the bed to face her. "Tell me why you stabbed a man to death."

"I fucked up." She scoots up the bed and rests against the headboard. "I drank too much and misread the situation in the morning. I reacted, he died. End of story."

I stare at her in an effort to evaluate her truthfulness. She's not necessarily lying, but she's leaving out a whole lot of detail.

"And?"

"And what?" she snaps. "I told you, end of story."

"Maybe his death is the end, but the story isn't complete."

Sylvia wraps her arms around her knees and hunches her shoulders. I move from my bed to hers to sit next to her. I don't touch her, but I want to. I want to assure her that she can tell me anything. I want her to know I'm not judging her or her actions. I don't give a shit what happened that night other than in the interest of how it impacted her.

"Tell me the rest, Sylvia."

She turns her head, and her eyes lock onto mine. There's a sheen to them, one that tells me she's on the verge of losing it. And if I know anything about this woman it's that she doesn't like showing weakness. So whatever information she's leaving out is big.

Sylvia swipes at the lone tear that breaks free and sighs. "We met at a bar that night. I spotted him across the room and thought he'd looked perfect for a one-night stand. That's all I was there for. Find a warm body to fuck and relieve some stress."

"Stress?"

"My mom and I had been fighting about Charlie. Not that that's anything new. But after our dad died, things got worse. And then everything with Leal came to light. Mom was understandably upset, but she started babbling about having suspicions and not doing anything about them to protect her daughter." Sylvia takes a deep breath before continuing. "And there I stood, taking it all in, and learning for the first time that she could have protected me too."

Sylvia rests her head on my shoulder as if she can't physically hold it up anymore.

"Anyway, we got in a big fight about Charlie being the favorite, and I left with one thing on my mind: fuck my cares away. Finding someone and forgetting everything, even if just for a few hours, was my sole focus."

"I'm sorry."

"Don't." She grabs my hand and holds it close to her knees. "Don't feel sorry for me. Your pity is the last thing I want."

"Trust me, I don't feel pity. I just wish you didn't have the experiences you did growing up."

"Oh."

"Keep going with that night."

"Right." She takes a deep breath. "I spotted Todd—that was his name...Todd—I spotted him in the bar and made up my mind then and there. It didn't take long to convince him to take me home. We were both blitzed out of our minds." Her voice drops to barely above a whisper. "When we got back to his apartment, we drank some more. I was beyond wasted and probably should've slept on the couch, but that wasn't what I was there for. We went to bed and passed out."

"Right. You had sex and were confused in the morning."

I narrow my eyes in thought, unsure where this is going. I know she killed the guy, and while it might not be justified, I'm not learning anything new other than the fight with her mother."

"Not exactly," she says.

"Okay." I drag the word out.

"You're really going to make me tell you everything, aren't you?"

"No. But I'd like you to." I wrap an arm around her shoulders. "Whenever you're ready..."

Sylvia remains silent for so long I start to wonder if she's really not going to tell me the rest of what happened. Then she speaks, surprising the hell out of me.

"We didn't have sex."

I concentrate on giving no physical reaction to what she says, but it's hard.

"What?"

Sylvia pulls away from me and moves to the other side of the bed where she swings her legs over and stands. She grabs her bag and drops it on the mattress. After digging for a second, she pulls out a slim metal case and opens it.

"Do you mind?" she asks, showing me the joint in her hand.

"As long as you share." My tone is meant to tease, but I'm not sure if it translates. "I don't mind, Sylvia. Not at all."

She pulls a lighter out of her bag and lights the joint. Drawing on it, she holds in the smoke as long as she can before blowing it out. She passes it to me, and I take a hit, then another.

"When I woke up, my head was pounding, and I was still feeling buzzed. I couldn't remember where I was or how I'd gotten there. Everything was a blur, ya know? I was scared and it was only made worse when I realized I wasn't alone. We were both naked, and I freaked out. I searched for my clothes and found them next to the bed. I grabbed my knife from my jacket and just started stabbing him."

"You thought he'd raped you?" It's a question I already know the answer to, and I'm validated when she nods. "But you said you didn't have sex."

"We didn't," she confirms. "After I stabbed him, memories of the previous night came rushing back."

"But it was too late because he was already dead."

"It wasn't too late." She grabs the joint and takes another hit before passing it back to me. "When I realized that I was wrong, that we didn't sleep together, I could have stopped. I *should* have stopped. But I didn't, I couldn't. I kept stabbing. He fought for his life, and I didn't stop. I was so fucking angry at the world that it was no longer Todd I was killing. It was my mom, Charlie, Leal... everyone but Todd."

Sylvia breaks down and begins to cry. I try to hand her the joint, but she refuses, frantically shaking her head.

"He didn't do anything wrong, and I killed him. I

slaughtered him, and he was just a guy in a bar. He was a nobody."

Sylvia collapses on the bed and curls into a ball. She sobs as if her heart is being ripped from her chest. I shift across the mattress so I can wrap her in my arms and hold her. I have no idea how long we lay there, but I let her cry until she's all cried out.

She rolls over and faces me. "Please don't tell anyone," she pleads. "I didn't give Donovan the full story when I called him. I couldn't. He, along with everyone else, already thought I was a fuck up."

"Shh." I run my hand through her hair. "I'm not going to tell anyone."

She exhales forcefully, as if she was waiting for me to say that, worried that I wouldn't.

"You really don't think less of me?"

I chuckle but there's no humor in it. "Sylvia, I've spent the last however long on a hunting spree, picking off men who have a connection to a cult. The only information I know for sure is that those who die *are* connected. And when I'm watching the life drain from their eyes, I feel euphoric. The only thing you could do to make me think less of you is be a part of the Church."

Sylvia lifts her head and looks at me with curiosity. "Why didn't you bring in your brothers? Why do it all alone?"

I'm surprised by her question. There are so many more she could have asked, but instead, she chose the one question that's at the heart of the matter.

"They're family," I say simply.

"Which is exactly why you should have told them."

"Like you told yours?" I counter, although I don't expect a response. Hurt flashes in her eyes, so I decide to answer her question. "I didn't tell them because it's my fault the Church ever came onto the club's radar in the first place. I was trying to protect them, protect my sister."

"Yet here we are."

I pull Sylvia into my side and urge her under the blanket, trying to buy myself time before admitting she's right. I don't regret what I did. Hell, I don't even feel bad about it. But it didn't stop the evil from showing right back up at the club's doorstep. It didn't stop Sylvia from getting hurt. It didn't stop a damn thing.

"Yeah, here we are."

Chapter Seventeen

Trainwreck is going to take one look at me, and he'll be as uncomfortable as I am.

Sylvia

"Brick seems to be keeping his distance today."

We're four hours into the second day of our trip and stopped at a rest area to stretch our legs. I look over my shoulder and see Brick talking to Donovan and Fender, and then I return my gaze to Trainwreck.

"Sure is."

I stifle a yawn but not before Trainwreck sees it, and when he chuckles, I reach across and slug him in the arm. He rubs the spot and pretends it hurts.

"What was that for?" he asks.

"How are you so damn chipper? You got the same amount of sleep I did and I'm fucking tired."

Trainwreck shrugs. "I've got a lifetime of sleepless nights under my belt, so I guess I'm just used to it."

"I've got plenty of them too, but I still require more than three hours of rest to feel remotely human."

"I'll be sure to keep that in mind."

Out of the corner of my eye, I see Fender and Charlie walking toward the building, Donovan not far behind. I try to keep my attention on Trainwreck, but something makes the hair on the back of my neck stand up. I feel like I'm being watched.

I twist to look all around me, and I see Brick again. He's staring at me but standing with Royal next to my bike. I've kept an eye on the prospect, and so far, have no concerns about him with my Harley. He's a damn good rider and treats my Harley as if it were his own. I'm glad I chose him.

Royal is laughing at something Brick said, yet Brick still doesn't appear one hundred percent engaged in the conversation. There was a time I'd have felt empowered by his seeming inability to focus on anything but me. Now I just want to add to his bruises for it.

"Ignore him, Syl."

I whirl back around, fully expecting Trainwreck to be staring at me, but his eyes are trained on the same thing mine were.

"Like you are?"

He shifts his gaze to me as he walks around his bike. When he pulls me in his arms and buries his nose in my neck, I can't stop myself from giggling. Right there in the rest area parking lot, I giggle like a teenage girl who's skipping class and contemplating second base with her boyfriend under the bleachers.

"Is that better?" he asks just before nipping at my flesh.

"Much."

"Do you have any idea what I want to do to you?"

I shake my head, completely crumbling under the growl in his voice, the way it rumbles against me.

"If it were up to me, I'd bend you over backward on my

bike and bury my face between your legs. I'd trace your folds with my tongue until you're quivering. I'd wait until you're on the brink of exploding and—"

"Let's ride!"

Trainwreck and I separate quickly at the sound of Fender's command.

"Kill joy," I mutter under my breath and Trainwreck simply shakes his head at me.

"Later."

His voice is full of promise, and I find myself mentally counting down the minutes for the rest of the day's drive. We don't stop as much as the first day, instead grabbing food from vending machines at the next rest area. And when we reach the hotel, we're all a little tired and out of sorts.

Unlike last night, we are all staying in the same hotel. Fender and Charlie get everyone checked in and pass out keys. This time, Charlie hands me my own.

"Thanks."

She presses the key into my palm and squeezes my hand for a second. "You're welcome."

We smile at each other, both genuine smiles that I don't think either of us have felt for a long time. Maybe I'm able to now because I got a lot of shit out of my system when talking with Trainwreck. Or maybe it's just because she's my sister and nothing will ever change that. Whatever the reason, I find I like it. It's hard work keeping up with a grudge.

"Can I come to your room in a bit?" she asks me.

I glance at Trainwreck, who's patiently waiting to walk me inside, and then I move my eyes back to Charlie. "Sure." I pull my cell out of my pocket and check the time. "Give me an hour to grab a shower first?"

Charlie nods. "See ya in an hour."

She continues passing out keys, leaving me alone with Trainwreck. He grabs both our bags and extends his arm. I dip under it and lean into him while we walk inside toward the elevators.

"What's your room number?" I ask.

"Six oh four. You?"

"Six oh five. We should be right across from each other." My lips tilt into a grin. "Thank you, Charlie."

Trainwreck laughs as we step onto the elevator. The sexual tension between us sizzles on our way up to the sixth floor. The elevator jolts to a stop, and the doors slide open. We follow the sign pointing to the left, toward our rooms.

As we walk down the hall, the tension builds, but I shove it aside. I want Trainwreck like I want my next breath but definitely not when there's a threat of Charlie interrupting. There's no way an hour would be long enough.

Trainwreck takes the key from my hand and unlocks my door for me. I quickly push it open and turn to face him. I press a hand to his chest to stop him from trying to come in.

"Wanna grab a drink at the bar later?" I ask.

His face falls with disappointment. "Yeah, sure."

"Tyler, this isn't a brush off." I rise onto my tiptoes and press my lips to his cheek, close to his ear. "I'm holding you to your promise of later."

I feel his cheek move with the lift of his lips. "Later," he repeats.

I pull back and lock eyes with him. "Yep. When we have no interruptions."

"Got it." Trainwreck kisses me on the cheek and turns around to unlock the door to his room. Before stepping inside, he tosses a glance over his shoulder. "Get me when you're ready to go to the bar."

His door shuts behind him, and I close mine. I toss my

bag on the bed to dig through it for clothes and pull out clean jeans and a hoodie. I don't know if a hotel bar counts as a date, especially when we've been together non-stop for two days, but I definitely don't want to meet him smelling like the road.

My shower is quick. Nothing like it was last night when we stopped. I put on the bare minimum of makeup, just enough to highlight my eyes and disguise my wind-reddened cheeks.

As I'm putting my dirty clothes in my bag, there's a knock on the door. I open it, and Charlie shoves a beer at me.

"Here," she says. "Peace offering."

I take the beer and step aside for her to enter. She flops herself on the bed and then scoots into a sitting position against the headboard.

"Make yourself comfy," I mumble.

"Thanks, I did." She grins and pats the bed beside her. "C'mon, sit down and kick your feet up."

I do as she says. For a split second, I berate myself for doing what I'm told, but I quickly move past it. I'm not sitting because she told me to. I'm sitting because I want to.

"Are you wearing makeup?"

I chug down half of my beer. "Yep."

"Aw, you got all prettied up for me." Charlie bumps my shoulder with hers.

"Not for you," I clarify on a laugh.

Charlie twists her head to look at me, her eyes wide like a thought just occurred to her. "Oh my God, am I being a cock blocker?"

I open my mouth to lie, but something stops the words from coming out. It doesn't take a genius to figure out what. I don't want to lie to her or fight with her anymore. The damage we've already done to our relationship is immense, and rather than aggravate it, I want to repair it.

"Not yet." I settle on the very basic truth.

Charlie stares at me for a moment before relaxing her body. "Trainwreck's a good guy." Her eyes light up. "And I bet he's a fucking stallion in bed. The loner types are always surprising."

I almost choke on my beer. "Jesus, Char." I swipe at my mouth.

"What?" Her tone holds a mixture of innocence and sisterly teasing. "Am I wrong?"

"Well, no. I mean, I haven't slept with Trainwreck yet, so I don't know about the whole stallion thing. But yes, loner types can be a surprise in the sack."

"I think it's all that time spent in isolation or whatever." She waves her hand flippantly. "It's like a parent who stays home to take care of the kids. When they finally get some adult time, they go a little wild. With loners, when they let themselves be with another person, they make the most of it."

"And Trainwreck is a loner?"

"You can't be that blind, Syl. Of course he is. Look at everything he did trying to take out the Church. All alone. He puts on a good front for parties and stuff. And he's loyal as fuck to the club. But he spends most of his time alone if he can help it."

I think back over the time that has passed since he carried me out of that cage. Charlie's right. Trainwreck likes to be alone. He's spent the majority of his time with only me, unless it's something to do with the Church or the club. He doesn't hang around with his brothers much. I have no doubt that he likes being with them, but he chooses not to be.

"Anyway," Charlie begins, pulling me back to the moment. "He's a good guy. Do you remember how he was when he was prospecting?"

I can't stop the snort that escapes. "Yes. He reminded me of that prospect on Sons of Anarchy. Oh, what was his name?"

"The one in the beginning with the deer head?"

"Yes, that's him," I confirm. "Trainwreck definitely earned his road name. But he's come a long way."

"Fuck yes, he has. He's one of the best members I've seen patched into a club. I'd trust him with my life." She smiles at me. "I trust him with yours."

We sit there in silence for a few minutes. I can't tell what Charlie's thinking, but my own thoughts are loud. Every fight we've ever had, everything I've ever blamed her for runs through my head.

Charlie is the first one to break the silence. "I'm sorry I've been such a bitch."

And therein lies the problem. Charlie has been bitchy, but Trainwreck helped me see, or start to see at least, that it's from a good place. And I certainly haven't helped matters.

"You don't need to apologize for being a big sister, or for trying to protect me. I get it, Char. I really do."

"I'm glad, but I need you to know that it isn't because I think you're a child or because I don't trust you. I do." She takes a deep breath and exhales before continuing. "Fender and I had a long talk last night. We both feel really bad for how we've treated you. You're an amazing, strong, independent woman, and you deserve to be treated as such. I just feel like it's my job to keep you safe, and clearly I haven't done that."

"It's not your job, Char. It never was. It was Mom and

Dad's job to keep us both safe, to teach us how to stand on our own two feet. They taught us well."

I don't talk about how they didn't protect me like they didn't protect her. I don't talk about the fights I've had with our mother. Maybe someday I will, but right now, we're making progress, and I don't want to do anything to jeopardize that.

Charlie leans close and pulls me in for a hug. "I love you, Syl."

"Ditto."

My sister huffs out a breath and leans back to look at me. "Now that that's over, we've got work to do."

"What are you talking about?" I ask, confused.

"If you're meeting up with Trainwreck tonight, which I know you are so don't try to tell me otherwise, you need a different outfit."

"But I like my jeans and hoodie. They're comfortable. And Trainwreck doesn't care."

"He may not mind, but that doesn't mean he also wouldn't mind something a little more... revealing. Something sexy. The goal is to get him in bed to have sex, not take a nap."

An hour later, I'm wearing a completely different outfit and more makeup than I've worn because I wanted to in a long time. I may not be comfortable, but I don't mind.

Trainwreck is going to take one look at me, and he'll be as uncomfortable as I am.

Chapter Eighteen

She could very well be the death of me.

Trainwreck

Two phone calls, a shower, and a joint and a half later, there's a knock on my door. I force myself to cross the room slowly, so I don't come off as too eager. But the fact of the matter is, I am, and I'm not sure I can completely hide it.

My jaw drops when I open the door. Saliva pools under my tongue, and my heart races. Sylvia is wearing her usual tight jeans, but instead of her riding boots, she's wearing black leather ones that lace up to just above her knees. There is no hoodie in sight, but rather a dark green top that buttons up the middle, leaving hints of flesh exposed while hugging her curves and pushing her tits up to taunt me.

Sylvia glances down at herself and frowns. "I knew this was a stupid idea."

She starts to turn back toward her room, but I grab her

hand and yank her into my room. She slams against my chest.

"There's nothing stupid about it." I grab the top of her shirt and tug it down, exposing a peaked nipple. I roll it between my fingers and revel in the way she presses hard against me. "Do we have to go to the bar?"

"Mmm," she moans. "I want to say no but can't. I thought it would just be the two of us, but it turns out, everyone is going to be down there. It'd look weird if we weren't there."

"I'm okay with weird."

Sylvia grabs my head and lifts it up so I'm looking her in the eyes. "I am too." She presses a kiss to my lips but pulls away before I can deepen the kiss. "Which is why we aren't staying long."

With that, she puts her shirt back into place and grabs my hand to tug me out the door. I pretend to drag my feet but in reality, it'll be nice to have a few beers with my brothers. Hell, I don't even mind drinking a few with the Black Savages.

When we step off the elevator onto the first floor, the sound of rowdy bikers reaches us. I glance around the lobby and make note that the only other people are the desk clerk and a middle-aged gentleman sitting in a chair reading a book.

"There you are." Greaser comes through the doorway to the bar and salutes us with a beer. "I was wondering when you'd show your face."

"You're drunk," I accuse, but I laugh as I say it.

"That I am, brother, that I am."

Sylvia and I lunge forward when Greaser trips over his own feet and catch him before he hits the floor.

"Isn't it your night to watch the van and Bartholomew?"

I narrow my eyes at him. "How are you gonna do that if you're passed out drunk?"

"I talked Piston into doing it." Greaser's words slur. "He's in a mood and said he could use the excuse to work out some aggression." Greaser leans forward and puts a hand up next to his mouth like he has a secret. "Between you and me, I think he misses his ol' lady. As soon as he's home and gets laid, he'll be fine."

Sylvia throws her head back and laughs. When she sobers, she and I guide Greaser back into the bar and leave him on a stool in the hope that he can't get into too much trouble there.

"Is he always like that?" she asks as we're walking toward Fender and Charlie.

"When my sister isn't around, or he isn't in 'dad' mode..." I shrug. "Pretty much."

"Seriously?"

"No, not really. Greaser's a good guy. He likes to party, but he's mellowed a lot since he and Trinity got together. Don't get me wrong, he has no problem doing whatever needs doing or getting lit with the rest of us. But he doesn't go looking for trouble anymore. He's got a wife and son to think about now."

"Makes sense."

"Now, can we stop talking about my brother-in-law?" I stop walking and turn her to face me. "We've got others to see, beers to drink, and a room to get back to."

Sylvia slaps me in the chest playfully. "Is that all you're thinking about? Getting back to the room and having your way with me?"

"Since the second I opened the door and saw you standing there in that." I nod at her outfit.

We spend the next hour or so having a few beers and

downing a couple of shots. The mood among the group is mixed. Some are letting loose and having a good time while others are standing around talking about the next forty-eight hours and our plan.

I order myself another beer and watch as Sylvia talks with her sister and Donovan. She's laughing, as are they, and I can't help but feel glad. Charlie is her blood family and Donovan? Well, he's her family too.

All my good feelings disappear when Brick joins the three of them and tries to wrap his arm around Sylvia's waist. Donovan says something to him, and he backs off, but doesn't walk away. I set my beer on a table and start toward them. When I'm about half-way there, Sylvia hugs her sister and heads in my direction.

"Ready to go?" she asks when she reaches me.

I give one last look in Brick's direction before focusing solely on Sylvia and the night ahead.

"More than ready."

We make it to the elevator, and the second the doors slide closed, Sylvia jumps up, giving me no option but to catch her. She wraps her legs around my waist and fuses her lips with mine. The doors open, and we don't bother to break apart.

I carry her down the hall, never breaking the kiss. Her tongue glides past my lips as I steady her in my arm, and I reach for my key card. It takes three tries for me to get the door to unlock, and I'm so frustrated by it, I kick the door open when it finally gives the right beep.

"Someone's impatient," Sylvia teases.

"Aren't you?"

"Very."

Sylvia hops free of me and struts toward the bed. My eyes are glued to her ass, to the way her hips punctuate every step. Her knees hit the mattress, and she slowly turns around to face me. She crooks her finger, and I waste no time closing the distance between us.

I toe off my boots while she works on my belt. By the time my feet are free, she's shoving my pants over my hips. I kick them off and to the side. Sylvia's fingernails trace a path up my chest as she lifts my shift over my head and tosses it to the floor.

"What about you?" I ask.

Sylvia spreads her arms wide. "Have at it."

Oh, this is going to be a wet dream come true.

I grab the low-cut hem of her shirt, just between her tits, and rip it off of her, sending buttons flying. She's not wearing a bra, so I dip my head and suck a nipple into my mouth to swirl my tongue around it. While I keep that up, alternating from one side to the other and back again, I unbutton her jeans. My fingers brush lacy material, so I grab that and her pants to push down her legs. They don't go far because they get caught up on her boots.

I release her nipple with a pop and trail my tongue down, over her stomach until I reach her center. Inhaling her scent, I brush past the part of her I want to taste the most and focus on getting those damn, sexy boots off.

Gripping her hips, I push her backward, so she sprawls on the bed. I unzip one boot, then the next, and tug them off her legs before tossing them over my shoulder to hit the floor with a thud.

I finish undressing her, and by the time she's naked, my cock is hard and begging to be swallowed up by her pussy. But not yet. I'm going to take my time with her.

I stand up and lean over her to nip at her lips, her neck, her collarbone. Sylvia's arms press against my shoulders, urging me lower.

"Mouth, pussy, now," she orders, her breathing getting choppier the lower I go.

"Yes, ma'am."

Settling between her thighs, I use my shoulders to push her knees apart as far as I can. Her scent invades my senses. I inhale deeply, as if that will somehow lock her inside my body for all eternity. I touch the tip of my tongue to her clit for a split second, and her hips buck.

"Mmmm," she moans.

Unable to hold back or tease her any longer, I lap at her core, darting my tongue in and out, and savoring the taste of her. Her hips continue to buck, almost as if she can't control it. Rather than try to urge her to stay still, I thrust two fingers into her pussy and feed her thirst for more.

Sylvia's legs begin to shake as I continue to finger fuck and eat her like a starving man. Her knees clamp tight around my head, and her feet hit my back as she drapes her legs over my shoulders.

"Oh fuck... mmmm..."

Her moans barely register as I lose myself in her. I growl against her, sending vibrations through her clit, and her pussy starts to clench. Rather than let her come, I remove my fingers and mouth and rise up to look at her face.

"No," she cries. "Don't stop. Why'd you stop?"

I slowly crawl up her body, sucking her juices off my fingers as I do, and stop when I'm centimeters away from her lips.

"I'm not ready to let you come yet."

I wrap my arms around her body and roll us both over so she's straddling me. Sylvia tries to lift herself up, but I don't let her. My cock is begging me to let her take over and impale herself on me, but I take a few deep breaths to calm myself.

"I need to come, Tyler," she says as she moves so she's practically sitting on my face. She lowers herself, and I breathe her in. "I need to come now."

I tease her clit for a few seconds before using whatever strength I have that isn't being used to keep myself from exploding and flip her around so we're facing away from each other. Pushing gently against her back, I ease her face toward my dick. Sylvia knows exactly what I want.

She wraps her lips around me, and I can't stop myself from thrusting deep, touching the back of her throat. When she hums, I almost lose it. Sylvia lowers her hips, and I suck her clit into my mouth, mimicking her movements on my cock as best I can.

I wish I could say we go at it for hours like this, but in reality, it doesn't last long. We both have too much desire pent up and need release. Sylvia sucks me off like a champ, and my spine begins to tingle. I wait for her to shift away from my dick, but she doesn't. Instead, she increases her speed until she's swallowing every last drop of cum that shoots into her mouth. At the same time, her hips tense and I grip them tight while her cunt coats my tongue.

Sylvia collapses on top of me, her legs still spread around my face. Her skin is slick with sweat, as is mine, and the room smells like sin and sex. My cock springs back to life, and Sylvia tosses a look over her shoulder.

"We're not done, are we?" Even though she asks the question, her tone gives off nothing but hope.

"Not by a long shot."

Once again, I flip her over onto her back and shift so I'm above her. She reaches between our bodies and grips my cock, pumping up and down. Every few strokes, she releases my length to roll my balls in her fingers, and it's then that I realize, she could very well be the death of me.

What an incredible way to go, though.

"Fuck me, Tyler," she pleads. "For the love of God, fuck me."

I shove her hand out of the way and line myself up at her entrance. Sylvia doesn't give me time to thrust as she lifts her hips, and I glide into her until my balls slap her ass. She's wet, hot, tight around my cock.

Thrusting in and out of her, in and out, I squeeze my eyes closed for a second before opening them so I can see what I'm doing to her. So I can see my own ecstasy mirrored in her gaze. But I can't see, because her lids are closed.

I brush a hand over her cheek. "Open up those brown beauties and look at me." Sylvia slowly opens her eyes and stares at me. "That's better."

Sylvia picks up the pace, her hips banging into mine. Thrust for thrust, we stay together in a rhythm that makes my muscles burn.

My balls begin to tighten, my spine tingles. I reach between us and rub fast circles around her clit.

"Come for me, Syl," I growl.

Sylvia's body tenses for a split-second before her pussy spasms around my dick. The spasms increase, and I can't stop the freight train that barrels through me.

"Fucking hell you feel so good."

I never take my eyes off of her. We watch each other as we both shoot into the sky and explode like firecrackers, only to float back to Earth together.

When we're spent, I roll to the side so I don't crush her and pull her into my arms.

Sylvia tucks her head under my chin and throws an arm across my chest.

"You really are a stallion," she whispers.

Trainwreck chuckles but there's a hint of self-consciousness in it.

"What?"

Sylvia yawns and makes no effort to hide it. She twists and sticks a leg between mine.

"It's a good thing, Tyler." I feel her lips lift into a sleepy smile. "Just go with it."

Chapter Nineteen

This can't be happening. Not twice in one day. This is no coincidence.

Sylvia

Sun streams through the curtains, and I throw an arm over my eyes to block it. When that doesn't work, I pull the blanket over my head. That helps with the light, but it does nothing to block the incessant pounding outside the room.

"Make it stop," I whine.

"I could, but it wouldn't be pretty."

I sit up at the sound of Trainwreck's voice and almost bang my head on his.

"Whoa, sleepyhead." He plants a kiss on my lips. "No need to be giving us both a concussion."

"Sorry," I mumble, still not quite awake. "I don't remember falling asleep last night. I guess I thought I was in my room." The pounding continues. "What the hell is that?"

"That would be someone else who thinks you're in your room."

"What?"

I get up and walk across the room. Just as I grab the knob to open the door, Trainwreck rests a hand on my arm to stop me.

"You probably don't want to do that."

"Why?"

"Because you're naked."

I glance down at myself and groan. Jesus, I really don't function well on such little sleep. Since I can't open the door, I look through the peephole, and fury hits me so hard, the fact that I'm tired is forgotten.

"What the fuck is he doing?" I ask, more to myself than anything.

Bang, bang, bang. Brick continues to pound on my door as if that will make me suddenly appear.

"I'd say he wants to see you about something."

"Thank you Captain Obvious," I mutter. "I'm going to have to have a talk with Donovan. He's gotta make this stop. He's walking a thin line between someone who can't take a hint and someone who's working their way up to stalker status."

"Do you want me to talk to Brick?"

"What?" I shake my head. "No. That would only make it worse."

"If you change your mind, all you gotta do is say so."

"Thanks. Seriously though. I've told him we're over so many times. I hate asking Donovan for help, but I don't see what choice I have. Maybe if his president issues an order, he'll finally get the hint."

"Maybe."

Trainwreck doesn't sound convinced and that leaves a pit of worry in my stomach. I'm not concerned about Trainwreck. No, I'm worried about Brick. He's never been like this, that I've seen, so I can't help but wonder: Why now? Why me?

The pounding finally stops, and footsteps thud down the hall as Brick walks away. I cross the room and snag the long-sleeved T-shirt Trainwreck was wearing last night and pull it over my head. It hangs almost to my knees, which suits me perfectly.

"I'm gonna grab my shit from my room and bring it over here." I pick up my jeans from last night and take the key card out of the back pocket.

Without waiting for a response, I open the door and peek around it to make sure Brick is gone. He is, so I rush across the hall and swipe my card. It takes me less than five minutes, and when I return to Trainwreck's room, the shower is running.

Making up my mind, I take off his shirt and make my way toward the bathroom to join him but am stopped by the sound of my cell phone ringing. I backtrack and pick up the device from the nightstand and see that it's Charlie.

"Hello."

"Where are you?"

"At the hotel, same as you."

"Oh, thank God." She lets out a sigh. "I heard Brick talking to Donovan in the hallway, and he said something about you being missing. I got worried."

"Brick needs to get a grip. He pounded on my door forever."

"Why didn't you answer?"

"Because I wasn't there." I pause, and Charlie inhales,

gearing up to ask another question. I continue before she has a chance. "I stayed in Trainwreck's room last night."

"Was I right?" Her tone is giddy. "Is he—"

"Total stallion."

"I knew it."

I hear Fender in the background but can't make out what he's saying. What I do hear is Charlie saying, "Trainwreck's a total stallion."

Fender must be closer now because I can make out his next words.

"Fuck, Char, I did *not* need to know that."

"Then don't listen to my conversations."

"Yo, Charlie," I bark, trying to pull her attention back to the phone call. "Back to Brick. Did Donovan believe that I was missing?"

"Don't know, but I don't think so. I'd say no if he hasn't come to check on you."

"Well, he hasn't so…"

"Listen, I just called to make sure you were okay. But I need to grab a shower because we leave in thirty. See you in a few."

Charlie ends the call, and I glance at the time. Holy shit, she's right. It's almost seven thirty. We're supposed to leave at eight. Trainwreck steps out of the bathroom, and I can't help the disappointment I feel when I see he's fully dressed.

"Shower's all yours."

"I think I'll skip it this morning. Don't really have time."

We spend the next fifteen minutes reviewing the route for the day and then head downstairs to the parking lot. It looks like we're still missing a few people, so we stash our bags and wait.

"Hey, Sylvia."

Royal jogs toward me, waving his hands as if I don't already see him.

"What's up?" I ask when he skids to a stop in front of me.

"Do you mind driving today?"

"Why can't you?" Trainwreck asks suspiciously.

"I can, but Fender asked me to drive the van so Bartholomew can be interrogated some more, see if he won't give anything else up before we get to Arkansas."

I glance in Fender's direction, and he's watching us. He nods, confirming Royal's reasoning.

"Yeah, I can drive."

"Thanks." Royal sounds excited, and then he looks at Trainwreck and his face falls. "Sorry, dude. Just following orders."

"Yeah, yeah. Get the fuck outta here."

Royal takes off and Trainwreck trains his gaze on me. "So much for feeling you all up against me today."

I pat him on the chest. "You'll live."

I turn to walk away, and he grabs me by the arm and spins me back around. Trainwreck kisses me, darting his tongue into my mouth to dance with mine. The kiss doesn't last long, and when he lets me go, he swats my ass.

"Stay close to me on the ride," he instructs.

"Or what?"

"Or nothing." Trainwreck shrugs. "I just want you close."

I laugh as I walk away from him, but then I spot Brick standing next to my bike and all laughter dies in my throat. What now?

"What do you want?"

"Is that any way to talk to family?"

"Brick, you're not my family. You're a club member and a guy I slept with once upon a time."

"That hurts."

"Well, you aren't getting the hint, so maybe hurting you is necessary."

"Is he why you wouldn't answer your door this morning?" he asks, tipping his head in Trainwreck's direction.

"That's none of your business," I snap. "And I didn't answer the door because I had nothing to say to you."

"Maybe I had something to say to you."

"What? What is so important that you had to bang on my door or bother me with it now?"

Brick glances around the parking lot as if to see who's watching. He settles his gaze on me again and shrugs.

"Nothing. It doesn't matter."

With that, he walks away with his head hanging. Maybe I shouldn't have been so hard on him, but he deserves it. He needs to figure out I can't be intimidated into giving him what he wants.

"Let's ride!"

I straddle my Harley and fire up the engine. The rumble beneath me helps to melt away my frustration with Brick. Trainwreck pulls up next to my bike.

"You okay?"

"I'm perfect now."

We pull out of the parking lot together, and we manage to stay side by side for the next three hours. Fender signals that we're stopping for a break, and the pack ahead of us takes the exit for the rest area.

As I start to turn my wheel and hit the brakes, my bike wobbles. Thinking it's just a rock in the tire or something, I get it back on track. I glance at Trainwreck, and he's watching me with worry in his eyes. Before I can even make sense of his look, there's a loud pop, and I lose all control.

Everything happens in slow motion. I point the bike toward the grass, so I don't hit any pedestrians at the rest area and to soften my landing when I go down. Because I *am* going to go down. As soon as I hit the area I'm aiming for, I lean over to lay the bike down and skid through the grass, tearing it up as I go.

I come to a stop just short of hitting a tree. I hear voices calling my name, but the pain is so intense, they're muffled and distant. I let my lids slide closed and pass out.

"Sylvia. C'mon Syl, open those brown eyes for me."

Who is slapping me?

"Please open your eyes."

I pry my eyes open, and Trainwreck's face is hovering over me. "Oh thank God." He breathes a sigh of relief. "What the hell happened?"

"I... I don't know." I wince at the pain in my leg as Trainwreck tries to help me sit up.

"Sylvia, your tire popped." Charlie comes into view. "Did you notice it low or anything before we left this morning?"

I shake my head. "No. I didn't make a point to look, but nothing jumped out at me."

Trainwreck lifts me off the ground and carries me toward the van. Fender is standing there, along with Donovan, Royal, and Brick.

"Damn, Syl," Donovan says as Trainwreck helps me into the front seat. "That leg looks nasty."

"Hurts like a bitch," I say from between clenched teeth. "I think it's just scraped to hell though from me sliding."

"Here." Brick hands me a lit joint. "This should take the edge off."

I inhale and let the smoke take hold. A couple hits and the edge is officially off.

"Thanks."

"No problem."

Brick leans against the van and finishes the joint.

"I'm so sorry, Sylvia," Royal says as he wrings his hands. "I didn't realize the tire was low. If I had, I'd never have let you on the bike."

"It's okay, Royal." I pat his arm. "Not your fault. Shit happens."

"It's the risk we take every single time we get on our bikes," Trainwreck agrees. "But if I ever have to watch that happen to you again, I'll take your Harley away."

"No, you won't."

"Oh no?"

"Not if you want to keep your balls," I threaten.

"You're right, I won't."

Our banter lightens the mood. Charlie helps me into the rest area so I can wash off in the bathroom. She bandages me up and we go back outside, me limping the entire way.

"Pretty sure you're not riding anymore today," Fender says when we reach the van.

"Definitely not," I agree.

Fender explains that they called a tow for my bike, and we'll be able to pick it up in the morning, once the tire is replaced. I trust that it'll be close to where we're staying so I leave it at that.

"I'll stay behind until the bike is picked up and catch up with you as soon as I can."

Fender and Donovan exchange a look and then Fender says to Brick, "Shouldn't be more than an hour or so, if their time estimate is right. You've got the address for the hotel, just in case?"

Brick taps the pocket of his cut. "Right here, in my phone."

"We'll see you later then."

It takes a few minutes to round everyone up, but it's not long before we're back on the road. I stare out my window from the passenger seat in the van and see Trainwreck sticking close. I wait for the annoyance to hit, the frustration that he's trying to protect me somehow, but it doesn't come. Instead, warmth floods my chest. I like his particular brand of protection.

I allow myself to drift off to sleep. I hate being in a cage, and this will make the time go faster. I don't know how long I'm asleep for, but I'm jolted awake by Squirrel slapping me from the driver's seat.

"What the hell, dude?"

The van swings from side to side.

"Put your damn seatbelt on!" Squirrel shouts.

It takes several tries because of the way I'm being tossed around, but the seatbelt finally clicks into place.

"What's going on?"

My window shatters, and a burning sensation tears through my shoulder. Squirrel howls in pain just as a hole is blasted through the front window.

"We're taking fire. I've been shot twice, and I'm not sure how much longer I can keep this thing under control."

Panic seizes my lungs. If we're taking fire, what's happening to the bikers out there in the open? I try to look out my window, but before I can get a fix on Trainwreck, the van starts to roll.

This can't be happening. Not twice in one day. This is no coincidence.

We roll a second time and then a third. The van comes to a jolting stop and the side is scrunched in from whatever it hit.

Bartholomew pleads for help from the back. Squirrel manages to get his seatbelt undone and then helps me with mine. When we're both free, we crawl out the windows because neither door will open. I start to run away from the vehicle, away from the smell of gasoline, but Squirrel goes to the back door instead.

"What are you doing?" I shout at him.

"We can't leave Bartholomew," Squirrel insists. "We need him now more than ever if we're going to figure out who attacked us."

I retrace my steps and help Squirrel try to get the door open. Nothing we do works. I spot a log a few feet away and pick it up to throw it through the window. I don't bother warning Bartholomew. Who gives a fuck if he gets a few more cuts?

Squirrel and I reach inside and drag Bartholomew out. Touching him makes my skin crawl, but I know it can't be helped. At least I get to inflict pain as we drag him across the jagged window glass.

We manage to drag him several feet away before the van explodes. I'm flung through the air like a rag doll, heat chasing me the entire way. When I hit the ground, the wind is knocked out of me, but trying to breathe proves difficult with the smoke surrounding me.

"Sylvia!"

Trainwreck!

"Where are you?!"

I'm right fucking here!

I try to inhale and throw myself into a coughing fit. I cough for so long, and so hard, my head starts to spin.

"Sylvia!"

"I'm..." Another coughing fit, more head spinning. "I'm right..."

The trees above me start to swirl around in the sky. I open my mouth to try and call out to Trainwreck, to call out to anyone who can hear me, but I pass out before any words pass my lips.

Chapter Twenty

Nothing.

Trainwreck

"Tyler."

I ring out the washcloth in the ice bucket and continue to wash the smoke, soot, and grit off of Sylvia's face. She's been moaning my name on and off since we got to the hotel. We had to stop earlier than we wanted but fortunately, Charlie was able to secure us all rooms.

"I'm right here," I assure Sylvia for what feels like the hundredth time.

"Squirrel?" Her eyes flutter open. "Is he...?"

"He's fine." I offer her my hand when she tries to sit up. "He's pissed off and will be sore for a few days, but otherwise, he's good. He and Piston went to find a computer store since all of his stuff was destroyed with the van."

"And..." She swallows. "What about Bartholomew?"

I knew this question would come. Squirrel said they

dragged Bartholomew out of the window, and he was alive. When we found him, the damage to his head suggests he hit it after the explosion.

"He's dead."

"What do we do now?"

"We adjust. Nothing is going to stop us from taking out the Church."

Sylvia nods curtly. "Good."

"I need to go meet with everyone, discuss what happened, figure out the new timeline since we didn't get as far today." I tuck a strand of hair behind her ear. "Do you want me to help you get a shower before I go?"

"No. I'll just get one in the morning."

"Do you need anything else?"

"Some ibuprofen and a glass of water would be great. I think I'll just crash until morning."

"Be right back."

I walk into the hall and call Fender. He answers on the first ring.

"How is she?"

"She's awake. Sore, tired." I run a hand through my hair as I envision how much worse she could be. "Hey, do you or Charlie have any pain meds... ibuprofen, Tylenol, whatever?"

The call becomes muffled, and I picture Fender with his hand over his phone. I hear him talking and he quickly comes back on the line.

"Charlie's bringing some up now."

"Thanks. I'll be down as soon as I get her settled."

"Have Charlie sit with her until she falls asleep. We need you down here."

"Got it, Prez."

I disconnect the call moments before Charlie steps off

the elevator. She strides toward me with a concerned look on her face.

"Is she okay?" she asks.

"She will be."

I open the door to Sylvia's room and let Charlie go in first. Sylvia is under the blanket on the bed and Charlie rushes forward to sit next to her.

"I'm fine, Char," Sylvia assures her. "Just a few bumps and bruises."

"Here." Charlie thrusts a few pills at her. "Trainwreck said you could use something to ease the pain. All I have is Tylenol, but I text Luna, and she's going to bring up something stronger in a bit."

Sylvia nods.

"I hate to do this," I interrupt. "But I really need to get downstairs and meet with the others. Charlie, do you think you can stay with Sylvia for a while? At least until she falls asleep?"

"I'll be fine," Sylvia insists before Charlie has a chance to answer. "You can both go."

"Sorry, Syl. President's orders," I tell her.

Sylvia groans but doesn't put up any more argument.

"I'll stay for a while," Charlie assures me.

"Thanks. I'll be back up as soon as I can."

"You guys, I'll be fine. Really. I'm just going to sleep."

"Then I'll stay until then," Charlie states. "Not a moment longer, I promise," she tells her sister.

Sylvia seems to think about it and nods. At least this way, she feels like she still has some control over the situation. And really, if she's just sleeping, she'll be okay.

Satisfied that I'm following orders, and that Sylvia isn't going to throw it back in my face that I don't trust her or think her capable of taking care of herself, I leave the room.

I make sure I take the key card though. I know I have my own room but there's not a chance in hell I'm staying there and not returning to Sylvia.

When I reach the first floor, I follow the noise and find the others in the hotel's conference room. They must have sweet talked the front desk clerk to open it for them.

"Finally," Fender says when I walk in. "We can get started."

I look around the room until my eyes land on Squirrel sitting at the table, surrounded by cell phones and computer equipment.

"What's he doing?" I ask Fender.

"Going through everyone's phone to see if he can figure out how we were tracked. Go ahead and give him yours."

"I didn't lead anyone to us," I argue.

"You don't think I know that?" Fender whispers harshly. "But I can't very well order everyone, including the Black Savages, to give up their devices and not demand the same of you. How would that look? Besides, I gave them mine as well, the second I got off the call with you."

I pull my phone out of my pocket and slide it across the table to the Squirrel. I don't like it but Fender's right. We need to figure this out, and I have nothing to hide.

Fender turns to Piston and nods.

"Shut the fuck up so we can get started!" Piston shouts to be heard above all the separate conversations taking place.

It takes a few minutes for everyone to settle down, but once they do, Fender has their undivided attention.

"Thank you," he begins. "I'm not going to talk long, as this is Trainwreck's show, but I appreciate everyone coming down to meet. It's been a long, fucked up day and I know we're all tired and pissed off. All I can say is hold on to that rage because you're gonna need it to get through the next phase of our plan."

Fender sits at the head of the long conference table so I can take over. I step next to his chair and look around the room, making a point to glance at every man.

"Fender's right. The rage is good. But it's going to take more than that to do what we have to do. Not only do we have our common enemy, the Church, but we now have a traitor among us." Voices rumble but I hold up my hand to quiet them. "You can speculate all you want but that gets us nowhere. Squirrel will figure it out by going through the phones."

"I don't see how it's any of us," a Black Savage complains. "We're all in this room. Don't you think if it were someone in this room, that person would have skipped this meeting?"

"That makes sense, yes, but it makes just as much sense for them not to skip the meeting so as not to draw suspicion. I'm not going to rely on any man's word." I nod to Squirrel. "The data will tell us what we need."

Squirrel hands several phones back to their owners. "You're cleared," he tells them as he does.

"As you all know, we didn't get to our final destination for the day. We still have about three hours to drive in the morning. We still launch our attack tomorrow night. At dark, we'll get into the compound, search for any victims and get them out. Then we blow some shit up, confirm casualties, and get the fuck out of there."

"Do you really think this Lord Luxuria is going to have victims on site?" Donovan asks. This isn't the first time he's brought up this concern and I get it. But we don't have time for him to second guess us.

"I do. There's a section of the compound that I've

confirmed through some of the men I've already taken out that he uses for *guests*. And by guests, I mean those women and children who have been kidnapped and are being trafficked as part of the yearly games the church plays."

"I still can't wrap my mind around how this happens so freely, so out in the open," one of the Black Savages says.

"Money can open a lot of doors, grease a lot of palms. This Church is ruthless and will do whatever it takes to continue to get away with it."

"And you're sure that taking out the main compound will stop them?"

"Listen up," Fender interrupts before I can answer. "We know this won't stop them, at least for a time. But the hope is to slow them down. Our attack will draw law enforcement and that will hopefully take out the rest of the organization. We know there's a chance that nothing will come of this other than a new leader taking power and building a new compound. We'll deal with that when the time comes."

"We?" Donovan asks.

"After this attack, the Black Savages' role in this will terminate. Remember, you're here for Sylvia. Beyond that, the Soulless Kings' can handle it," Fender clarifies.

"We'll ride at eight in the morning," I say, bringing the conversation back around to the mission at hand. "We'll meet again when we get to our final destination. We'll be going to the hotel we originally planned on staying at but only for the day. After the attack, we'll be driving as far north as we can. Everyone still on board, thump twice."

Two thumps fill the room as each man pounds either the table or the wall.

"Good. I suggest you all get some sleep. No one is to leave the property tonight, and there will be no partying.

We need to be sharp tomorrow." As everyone starts to rise and make their way to the door, I continue. "Someone will bring you your phones as you're cleared."

Men file out of the room, and I begin to follow but Fender stops me.

"T, you need to stay here with Squirrel while he continues to screen the phones."

"I need to check on Sylvia, Prez."

"Here, boss." Squirrel hands Fender his cell. "You're cleared."

"No shit, Squirrel." Fender chuckles and refocuses on me as he holds his phone up. "I'll check on her and text you. Your post is here until this is done."

With that, he walks out of the room, giving me no chance to argue.

"Might as well take a seat," Squirrel says. "It's gonna be a long night."

I can't sit so I pace instead. Ten minutes pass and a cell phone beeps from the pile on the table. I immediately search for one that has a screen lit up and see that it's mine.

Fender: Sylvia's sound asleep. Call me if you guys need anything.

I breathe a sigh of relief and respond with a thumb's up emoji. I toss my cell back into the pile and sit there, thinking, speculating... waiting.

"So, what exactly are you looking for?" I ask when I can't take the silence any longer.

"Anything suspicious really," Squirrel says. "Phone calls to known numbers of the Church. Phone calls to random numbers that stand out. Texts that don't conform to the user's norm. Deleted data. Basically, a needle in a haystack."

"And if you find nothing?"

"I'll find something," he assures me. "No one else knew about our plans, our route, but the people riding. Not even the ol' ladies back at home. There are no chapters of either club in Arkansas, so we don't have them to worry about." Squirrel locks eyes with me. "Don't worry, T. If there's something to be found, I'll find it. I promise."

I trust Squirrel when he says that. He's the *only* person I know who could find a needle in a haystack. There's just a lot riding on this and I find it difficult to relax. But I try.

For the next three hours I watch him work. He clears phone after phone and my worry deepens. When he finally clears mine, I dial Sylvia's number to check on her.

"Hi. You've reached Sylvia, and I'm too busy to answer your call. Leave a message, and I might call you back."

I hang up without leaving a voicemail. She must still be sleeping, which is good. I'm glad my call didn't wake her up.

Another two hours tick by, the clock on the wall taunting me with each jolt of the minute hand. My eyelids are getting heavy, and I know I need sleep as much as everyone else, but it's looking like I won't get any. It's already five o'clock in the morning and there are still at least ten phones to go through.

"Holy shit," Squirrel mutters, pulling me out of my stupor.

"What is it?" I ask, rushing to stand behind him and look at the computer screen. "Whose phone is that?"

"Get Donovan and Fender down here."

"Whose fucking phone is it?"

Squirrel looks at me, and the worry I see in his eyes makes my heart plummet to the floor.

"It's Brick's phone, T."

A blast of anger swirls through me before my body goes

cold, almost numb. I race from the room, but I don't wait for the elevator. I take the stairwell, two steps at a time, and burst through the door to the fourth floor.

Running down the hall to Sylvia's room, I silently pray I'm overreacting. My blood is pumping so hard, I hear it flowing through my veins, thumping in my ears.

I swipe the key card when I reach the door but I'm in so much of a hurry, it takes me several times to get it the reader to work. When I throw open the door, I freeze.

The room is empty. I rush through it to double check the bathroom. I yank the covers off the bed, almost convincing myself she's just tucked in real tight.

Nothing.

No Sylvia, no bags, no *hint* that she was ever here.

Chapter Twenty-One

What could I possibly have done to warrant this?

Sylvia

"And here I thought I gave you too much sedative."

I fight to keep my eyes open and roll toward the sound of Brick's voice. My movements are sluggish, my limbs heavy. I silently take in my surroundings and realize we're not at the hotel anymore. We're in *a* hotel room, but it's different from the one I fell asleep in. I open my mouth to speak, to shout for help, but Brick stops me.

"Ah, ah, ahh," he says. "No yelling. That'll draw attention to us and then I'll have to kill you." He holds up my cell phone. "And don't think you're gonna get a call out for help either."

"Kill me?" I croak.

"You're worth much more if I deliver you alive. I'd hate to lose all that money."

"Deliver me where?"

"You'll see... soon."

Brick walks to the mini fridge and pulls out a bottle of water. When he hands it to me, I don't take it. He huffs out a frustrated breath and unscrews the cap to take a drink.

"There, satisfied?" He sets the bottle on the nightstand next to the bed. "It's just water, babe."

I wait several minutes before my thirst gets the better of me, and I snatch the bottle to take a long, soothing swallow. When it's almost gone, the pain in my head and leg registers.

"Can I get some Tylenol or something? Please?"

Brick grabs a bag from the console that the television sits on and tosses it at me. "I figured you'd need something."

"Thank you." The words taste like acid on my tongue, but I know I need to play nice, at least for the time being.

"You said you gave me a sedative. What was it?"

"Does it matter?"

I shrug. "No, I guess not."

I glance around the room and see my bag on the chair next to the window. I don't know whether or not Brick has gone through my stuff, but I pray he hasn't and the knife Trainwreck gave me is still in there.

"Do you have any idea the trouble you've caused me?"

Brick's question pulls me back so my focus is on him. Trouble I've caused him? What could I possibly have done to warrant this?

I shake my head.

"It took me months to gain your trust, to get into your pants. I knew the second I did, I had you. But then you turned the tables on me, and I actually liked you." He gives a self-deprecating laugh. "I even thought about calling Pete off that night. But then you got all bitchy. Why'd you have to be such a horrible cunt?"

I try to wrap my head around what he's saying but can't.

Brick has been a world-class asshole lately, but he's a Black Savage. I can't believe he'd hurt me.

Look around, Syl. He clearly has no problems hurting you.

"Are you saying...?" I swallow hard. "You're the reason Pete took me?"

Brick smirks and for the first time, I see pure evil reflecting in his eyes. "Honestly, I thought Bartholomew would have spilled the beans in the Nightmare Room. He was such a stuck-up prick, always threatening to throw me under the bus if things went sideways. Imagine my surprise when he didn't."

My head is spinning with all of this new information. I think back to that night, to the party I left with Pete. I recall the things Bartholomew did say, how upset he was that it was me and not Charlie.

"I thought Charlie was supposed to be taken," I mumble. "It wasn't supposed to be me."

"Yeah, that's not exactly true." Brick crosses the room and sits on the mattress next to me. I try not to cringe at his closeness but it's hard. He disgusts me. "That's just what I wanted you to believe, to throw you off and keep the pressure off of me."

"So, are you...?"

Brick reaches into his back pocket and pulls out his wallet. He opens it and takes a card out to show me.

"Card carrying member of the Church of Sinfinite Opportunity." His tone tells me how proud of that he is.

"But why?" I shake my head as if that will make all the puzzle pieces fit. It doesn't. "You're a Black Savage. You grew up in the club. Why become a member of that cult?"

"It's not a cult," he barks as he backhands me across the face. "Don't ever call it that again." He takes a deep breath and seemingly calms himself down. "It's a way of life. A family." Brick shrugs. "The Church isn't all that different from the club."

I can't stop the snort that barrels out of my throat. "I doubt that."

"You don't believe me?"

"I have no reason to."

Brick stands from the bed and faces me before leaning down and boxing me in with his arms on either side of my head.

"You'll see, babe." He plants a quick kiss on my lips, so fast I don't even have time to react. "You'll see."

Chapter Twenty-Two

If he didn't want you to know, you weren't gonna know.

Trainwreck

"How the fuck did this happen?"

I watch as Fender and Donovan argue over who's at fault for Brick's actions and how we're going to get Sylvia back. We can't track her like we normally would. Squirrel already tried to track her phone, but just before he was able to narrow down a location, it was turned off.

"You tell me!" Donovan shouts.

"Brick is your guy, not ours," Fender counters. "This is on you."

"Stop!" I yell, tired of their fighting. It's not getting us anywhere. Both men look at me. "We can fight later about who's to blame. Right now we need to focus on getting Sylvia back."

"He's right," Charlie says as she walks up to us in the

parking lot of the hotel. "Fight later. Find Sylvia now." She focuses on Donovan. "Didn't you say one of your men saw Brick going into Sylvia's room?"

"Yeah." Donovan shrugs. "Not that it does us any good. He didn't think anything of it because of Brick and Sylvia's history. He thought they were just hooking up."

"Well they weren't," I snap. "Sylvia's with me."

"Trust me, I know." Donovan sighs. "She's made that very clear over the last few days."

"Good. Now help me get her back."

"What do you think I'm doing?" Donovan snaps. "I've got half of my guys trolling the town to see if they can find anything. The other half is here waiting on instructions."

"Then give them some," I bark.

"What should I tell them?" he counters. "We have no clue what direction they went. We don't know why he took her. We've got nothing!"

Just then, Squirrel joins the conversation. "Not exactly nothing. I've managed to trace a few of the numbers Brick was calling and all the phones were burners."

"Again, we have nothing."

"I was then able to determine where each burner was purchased," Squirrel says as if he weren't interrupted. "Get this." He flips his laptop around so we can see the screen. "Each of the three burners Brick had contact with was purchased in or around Lodge Corner, Arkansas."

"Where the Church compound is?"

"Yep." Squirrel snaps the lid closed on his computer. "I think he's taking her there. He's working for them."

"That's impossible," Donovan protests. "If he were part of a cult, I'd know it."

"Apparently not." Donovan opens his mouth to argue more but I hold a hand up to stop him. "Think about it.

He's been groomed his whole life to follow the rules of the club. And as we all know, a pretty big rule is not to reveal club secrets. He knows how to keep his mouth shut."

"Motherfucker! How did I not see this?"

"If he didn't want you to know, you weren't gonna know." I clap a hand on Donovan's shoulder. "It's not your fault."

"He's right," Fender agrees. "We're all masters at keeping secrets. He's just better than we thought."

I could continue to blame him, but the truth of the matter is, none of us saw it. We all trust our brothers, as we should. If you can't trust them, then you shouldn't be a member. But Brick fooled us all.

"He's gonna pay for it, that's for damn sure." Donovan shakes his head. "What now?"

Donovan is the president of a motorcycle club. He's used to calling the shots, making decisions on the fly. The fact that he's not right now, that he's giving up control, not to another MC president, but to me, a newly patched member, says a lot. The fact that he's trusting me, despite what his own brother, whom he's known for years, has done, says even more.

"We keep going in the direction we're going. We get our asses to Lodge Corner, Arkansas. My guess is she'll—"

My cell phone rings, and I pull it from my pocket. The number that flashes on the screen is unknown. I signal to Squirrel to trace the call and then answer it on the fourth ring.

"Hello."

"Let me guess," Brick says. "You've got that tech nerd of yours tracing this call."

I tap the speaker icon so everyone can hear.

"I wanna talk to Sylvia." I keep my voice calm and even. It's probably the most difficult thing I've ever done.

"Not gonna happen."

"Where are you?" Donovan asks.

"Oh, hey Prez. How's it hanging?"

"Cut the shit, Brick. Tell us where you are so we can come get Sylvia, and I'll give serious consideration to letting you go."

Brick laughs outright. "No you won't. We both know I'm as good as dead. Fortunately for me, you have to catch me first."

"I swear to fucking Christ, if you hurt her, it won't be Donovan and the Black Savages you have to worry about," I snarl.

"Hurt her? I'm not going to hurt her. I'm setting her up for life, man." He pauses. "Maybe not the best life, but better than she'd get with a punk like you."

I could go back and forth with him for days, but I know it's a waste of time. He's not going to give up any information.

"Just let me talk to her," I demand.

"I already told you, not gonna happen. The only way you're going to see your bitch again is if you outbid your competition. Right now, the going price is seven hundred and fifty thousand dollars." Brick chuckles. "So, Trainwreck, what's it gonna be? Exactly how much is Sylvia worth to you?"

I search my mind for a figure I think will satisfy Brick and that's when it hits me.

Everything. Sylvia's worth everything to me.

"Time's ticking. Tick, tick, tock."

With that, Brick hangs up. I whirl toward Squirrel.

"Tell me you got him."

Squirrel narrows his eyes. "I was able to confirm he's headed in the direction of Arkansas. He's on the move though. But as long as he keeps the phone on, I can keep the track going."

My phone beeps with an incoming text.

Tell the desk clerk thanks for the vehicle.

"Son of a bitch!"

"And we lost him," Squirrel says. "The phone is off."

"He took the desk clerk's car," I inform them. "That's how he's able to transport her."

"If he told you that, he's already ditched the vehicle. It's pointless to track it now."

Red haze clouds my vision as the rage in me builds. It's mixed with a desperate worry for Sylvia. I'm used to the rage. I know how to use that to my advantage. Worry is another thing entirely. I have to figure out how to let it fuel me, not slow me down.

"We leave in five," I snarl. "We're gonna find this fucker. And when we do, he's mine. Do you hear me? He's fucking mine."

Chapter Twenty-Three

Will I survive and get away or will I be forever in the hands of someone who owns me?

Sylvia

I lean against the window of the truck and pretend to be sleeping. We switched vehicles as soon as Brick was off the phone with Trainwreck so my hope of being found before we get to our destination dies a little.

"You hungry?"

I turn my head to look at Brick. Is he serious?

"It doesn't matter," he says. "I am."

Brick takes the next exit and turns into some local fast-food joint. He goes through the drive thru and orders us both food. I don't know that I can eat, but I'm going to try. I need something of substance in my stomach.

After he pays, he pulls away from the window. "Here." Brick tosses the bag into my lap. "Take what you want, and I'll eat the rest."

I dig through the contents and grab one of the three burgers and an order of fries. Brick didn't order drinks, but he hands me a bottle of water he snags from the floor of the back seat.

"We aren't stopping again, so don't drink too much."

I set the bag of the remaining food on the center seat and start to shovel my food into my mouth. I didn't realize how hungry I was until I smelled the burgers. Now, it's as if I can't get enough.

"That's one thing I've always liked about you," Brick says conversationally. "You've never been afraid to eat in front of a man. No salads and nibbling for you."

I wipe my mouth with the back of my hand.

"When you're done eating, you should try to take a nap. Things are bound to get crazy when we reach our destination."

The way he says destination almost sounds like he's taking me on a vacation. I heard him tell Trainwreck about an insane amount of money so it's more likely, he's selling me and going on a vacation himself. And he should if he wants to live. But he won't make it far if I have anything to say about it.

I finish my burger and fries and toss the trash into the bag. I know I won't be able to sleep, so I don't even bother to try.

"Can I ask you a question?"

Brick looks at me for a moment before nodding. "Sure."

"How'd you get involved in the Church?"

His eyes narrow but he keeps them on the road. "You really want to know?"

I couldn't care less but any information I can gather might prove useful, so I lie.

"Yes."

"Leal brought me into the fold."

Damn, this is deeper than I thought.

"Leal?"

"That's right," he confirms. "He always wanted to take the club in a different direction. That was a big issue between him and your dad. It started with you and Charlie. Although, Leal was stupid and couldn't give you guys up. Plus, he knew if he did, your dad would find out. So he kidnapped other children and sold them. He worked his way up the ranks of the Church. He was so well respected, he'd been invited to stay at the compound. By then, Leal had brought me into the fold, and he was going to take me as his guest." Brick scowls. "But your fucking sister and her old man made sure that didn't happen."

"They knew?"

"Of course not," he barks. "But he's still dead because of them. Anyway, it doesn't matter. Leal and I talked about what would happen if something happened to one of us. We made a pact that, no matter what, we'd carry on the legacy of the Church."

"And where does selling me come into play with carrying on the legacy?"

Brick shrugs. "It doesn't. Not really. That was more for my amusement than anything. And the money. I needed the money."

"And I was a horrible cunt?" I ask, repeating what he said earlier.

"That too."

The way he talks about all of this sends chills up my spine. He's callous, unaffected. Every move he's made, other than selling me, has been calculated. Despite what he says about needing the money and entertainment, the night I was taken was a whim. He said so himself. He was gonna call it off but got pissed at me and went through with it.

"Does knowing any of that make this easier for you?"

I don't know how to answer that. On the one hand, it doesn't because I know how ruthless and uncaring he is. On the other hand, it does because I'm fairly certain he doesn't want me dead. I have a chance at surviving this. The biggest question now is will I survive and get away or will I be forever in the hands of someone who owns me?

"I don't know," I respond.

For the remainder of the trip, we ride in silence. I have hundreds of questions but right now, I don't want the answers. I want to remain blissfully unaware of some things. As for Brick, I don't know why he's quiet. Planning his next move, maybe? Or mentally counting his financial windfall to determine just how far away from his own death he can get?

When we arrive at our destination, it's late afternoon. Based on our location last night, I thought we were closer, but I was wrong. We were all wrong. Of course, construction didn't help matters any.

"It's more impressive in person."

I glance at Brick before returning my attention to the mansion before us. The land surrounding it is dotted with buildings and houses for Lord Luxuria's staff. I know one of the buildings is where he keeps victims, but which one I can't be sure.

"It's something alright," I admit.

The double doors open at the entrance of the mansion, and two individuals step out. They're wearing matching uniforms, so I assume they're staff.

"And there's the welcome committee."

Brick sounds almost giddy as he gets out of the truck and walks around to open my door. He offers me a hand to help me out, but I ignore it. I refuse to give him the satisfaction or help him feel like a gentleman. He's anything but.

"Suit yourself," he says flippantly and turns to face the staff. "I believe our Lord is expecting us."

Oh my God. Lord Luxuria. A part of me knew Brick was bringing me to him, but I didn't want to believe it. Until about twenty minutes ago, I was still hoping the Soulless Kings and Black Savages would catch up to us and rescue me.

"Of course, sir," the man says.

"Please come in, and I'll show you to your rooms," the woman instructs. "Our Lord will be meeting you in the library in an hour."

Our rooms? Plural? Maybe this will be my chance to somehow get word to Trainwreck. I can reason with the woman. Surely she'll understand. Right?

"Follow me," she says.

We do just that. When we enter the foyer, I'm astounded by the amount of marble. Solid white marble to be exact. The place is pristine, stark, and decidedly feminine. Not at all what I would expect from a man who runs a cult. Maybe he's compensating for something or showing his true colors in a manner in which he can't out in the real world. Who the fuck knows?

"Sir, if you'll follow Mr. Doe, he'll show you to your room in the east wing," the woman says. "Ma'am, come with me. Your room is in the west wing."

Thank God there will be some distance between Brick and me.

Brick and Mr. Doe walk up a grand set of stairs and then disappear down the second-floor hallway.

"You called him Mr. Doe," I observe. "What can I call you?"

"Miss Doe, ma'am."

"Please, my name is Sylvia."

"I know, ma'am."

"Is there a phone in my room?" I ask, unable to wait and see for myself.

"Yes, ma'am."

"Perfect. Thank you."

Miss Doe stops in the middle of the hallway we're walking down and faces me. Her expression is one of concern.

"This is a blind spot, so I need to be quick. If we don't show up on the next camera when our Lord expects, there will be hell to pay." She glances over her shoulder as if expecting someone to pop out of the shadows. "There is a phone in your room. You can use it to make any call you like. But be aware, the calls are monitored, and the information gleaned will be used against you or anyone who comes for you."

"It's a chance I'll have to take."

Miss Doe turns away from me and starts walking down the hall again. She acts as if her words of warning were never uttered.

"You'll find a bathroom attached to your room. It's stocked with fresh towels, toiletries, and anything else you may need."

"I've heard that before."

"I'm sorry if you've been lied to during your journey here, ma'am. I can assure you, our Lord takes very good care of our guests."

The way Miss Doe says 'our' is odd, almost like she's a part of the cult and not a victim. I'm not buying it and anyone with half a brain wouldn't either. Even if she hadn't given me a warning, she's got victim written all over her, what with her uniform she no doubt had no say in, her name, which can't be her own. Maybe she's forced to say 'our', but there's something in the way she says it that I can't get out of my head. I can't shake the feeling that it means something important.

"Here we are, ma'am."

Miss Doe opens a door and ushers me into a gaudy room. More white marble but the decorations and furniture are not even close to on par with what I've seen up to this point. No, this room is full of cheap knockoffs and thrift store finds.

"Can I get you anything before I go?"

I turn to Miss Doe. "You said we're to meet Lord Luxuria in an hour in the library, correct?"

"That is correct, ma'am."

"How exactly do I get to the library?"

"Don't worry about that. I'll come and get you when it's time." Miss Doe grabs the doorknob. "If there's nothing else...?"

"I'm good. Thanks."

"My pleasure, ma'am."

Your pleasure my fucking ass.

The second the door closes, I race to the phone I spotted beside the bed. It's a rotary phone so I half expect it not to work when I pick up the receiver. Fortunately, a dial tone buzzes in my ear.

I dial Trainwreck's number, thanking the heavens that I know it. I'm good with memorization and phone numbers is something I make a point to commit to memory. Cell phones can't be trusted and growing up in an MC, I learned at a young age that anything can happen and access to a contacts list isn't always guaranteed.

"Hello?" Trainwreck sounds suspicious but just hearing his voice is like music to my ears.

"Tyler, it's me."

"Sylvia?"

"Yep," I confirm. "I'm at the compound. I don't want to say much just in case this call is being monitored."

"First, are you okay? If Brick hurt you, he—"

"I'm fine," I rush to interject. "He even fed me."

"That's something I guess," he mutters and then takes a deep breath. "Okay, give me what you can."

"I've got a meeting in an hour with the leader. From what I can tell, all intel is correct. But something is off."

"What?"

"I don't know. I can't quite put my finger on it."

"Okay. Do we need to adjust anything?"

I think about that for a moment. I can't give him the exact location of any victims, other than the staff if my suspicions are correct, but he didn't have that to begin with.

"No, not that I can tell. I have access to this phone, so I'll call if I need to."

"Understood."

"Just... I..." I heave a sigh. "Just be careful."

"Always." I can hear the smile in his voice. "And Sylvia?"

"Hmm?"

"You too."

Chapter Twenty-Four

Lives are riding on this.

Trainwreck

"She sounded good, right?"

I nod in response to Charlie's question. Sylvia did sound good. But I know better. These people are dangerous, some of the most dangerous I've come across. And Brick already knows he has nothing else to lose so there's no limit to what he'll do.

"We need to fill everyone in and get there though."

"I'll gather everyone up," Charlie says but she makes no move to do that.

"What is it?" I ask her.

"You really like her, don't you?"

"Yeah, I do." A lot. "But you need to know, even if I didn't, it wouldn't matter. I'd be doing the same thing to save her."

"No, T, you wouldn't."

"Of course I would."

"I have no doubt you'd do everything in your power to save anyone who needed it. But it's different when it's someone you care about." When I open my mouth, she holds up a hand. "I don't know if you love her or if the feelings will pass when this is all over. And really, it's not my place to figure that out. Just make sure you don't break her heart. Because if you do, I'll make it my place."

"I'm not going to hurt her. I promise."

"And T?"

"Yeah."

"Don't let her hurt you either."

Charlie walks away leaving me with something to think about. I can't say for sure if I love Sylvia or not. I know I care about her, about what happens to her. I know I want her to be happy and safe. I know my heart shattered into pieces when I saw the van explode and I thought she was in it. And the moment I saw she wasn't, it was whole again.

Is that love?

"Everyone's waiting on you."

I shift to see Greaser standing a few feet away, an expectant look on his face.

"I'm coming."

He turns to walk away but I stop him.

"Hey Greaser, can I ask you a question?"

"Sure."

"How do you know when you love someone?"

"I don't know, you just do." He shrugs.

"Bullshit. How did you know you loved my sister?"

Greaser pops his neck, clearly uncomfortable with this conversation. But I refuse to back off. I *need* to know.

"I knew I loved her when the thought of not having her in my life was unbearable. Love is when you care more about the other person's happiness above your own. When you realize that you would do anything for them, even if it costs you everything... that's love."

Greaser turns and walks away, and I'm left with the same question.

Is it love?

Do I care about Sylvia more than anything else? I know I'd risk my life for her. Would I risk my family, my brotherhood? Maybe not their lives, but my ability to be a part of them? Yes.

So, does that make what I feel love?

Maybe. Probably.

But whatever I feel won't mean shit if I don't have her back. With that in mind, I join the group and tell them what I know.

"Sylvia confirmed that our intel up to this point is correct. We've got many buildings on the compound, with one central mansion, where the new Lord Luxuria resides. There are victims on the property, other kidnapped and indentured individuals that need to be cleared from the property before we start our final attack."

"What about Brick?" Donovan asks.

"As far as I know, he's still there," I inform him. "If you want to punish him yourselves, since he violated your club's code, then get to him before I do. Otherwise, I make no promises."

"We're about an hour from the compound," Squirrel says as he hands out blueprints he had printed at a local library. "We're leaving in thirty minutes, which puts us there after dark as we planned."

"I thought we wanted to strike in the middle of the night?" someone questions.

"We did, but we can't afford to wait anymore. Sylvia's there and who knows how long that will last. Brick told us we could buy her but, if the Church's past is any indication, that's not even a remote possibility. Once they have someone, that's it. Time is up."

"If you don't like the plan, speak up now," Fender demands.

None of the Soulless Kings says a word.

"Same goes for Black Savages," Donovan states. "Sylvia is one of us. Brick was but he sealed his fate when he chose his loyalty to the Church over the club. If you're not on board with doing whatever is necessary to bring Sylvia home, turn in your patch and walk away."

Every last Black Savage remains in place.

"Good. Now let's get ready to ride!"

The group disperses until the only three remaining are Fender, Greaser, and me.

"You sure you can handle this?" Fender asks me.

"Why couldn't I?"

"Trainwreck, it's no secret that you have a thing for Sylvia. I just want to make sure your emotions aren't clouding your judgment." Fender claps me on the back. "If you can't, I'll take over, no questions asked. You've brought us this far, and we can take it from here."

"I can handle it, Prez," I assure him. "You're right, I have feelings for her. And that's exactly what makes me the best man for the job. I'll do anything to get her back."

"Told ya he was a goner," Greaser jokes.

"I figured. Just had to know for myself."

"Wait." I glance back and forth between the two of them. "This was some sort of test?"

"No. I'm being serious when I tell you there will be no consequences if you decide to back out, to wait for your girl. But I agree with you… feelings make all the difference in these situations. They give you drive, a purpose beyond revenge. Use your emotions if it helps. Just don't let them use you."

"And please don't get yourself killed," Greaser adds. "Your sister would never forgive me."

"In other words, there's a lot riding on this?"

"Lives are riding on this, T. So, yes, a lot."

Chapter Twenty-Five

I'm not the monster in this story.

Sylvia

"Don't make me shoot you... ma'am."

I look over my shoulder and see Miss Doe standing in my doorway, a pistol in her hand and pointed directly at me. The weapon is in stark contrast with her uniform and creates a sight that is contrary to her trying to help me earlier. I can see the laser above the barrel and glance down to see a red dot trained on my torso. If I were facing her, it'd be a fatal shot.

"Miss Doe, please."

I turn to face her fully, letting go of the sheet as I do. My plan had been to escape through the window after I made the sheet rope, but I must have triggered some sort of silent alarm.

"I don't like using guns, ma'am. It is required of me."

Miss Doe's voice is strained, and her tone suggests she's trying to explain her actions, as if that would help. In a strange way, it does. She's not going to kill me. Not unless I force her hand.

I hold my hands up. "No reason to use it then. I'm not resisting."

Miss Doe stares at me for a moment before her shoulders sag. She lowers the pistol and shoves it in the apron pocket of her uniform. How did I miss that earlier?

"Our Lord is waiting for you."

"Is Brick there yet?"

"Mr. Doe is escorting him to the library now."

"Any chance I can meet the Lord *after* Brick?"

I'll have a better chance of getting past Lord Luxuria if Brick isn't present. Brick is the one who can take me down. He knows most of my moves.

"No, ma'am."

"It was worth a try," I mutter to myself.

"Was it?" Miss Doe counters.

Rather than wait for an answer, she exits the room, only slowing down so I can catch up. As she leads me to the library, Miss Doe is silent, but fidgety. I can't help but wonder why, although I don't ask. Most people would be fidgety in this situation, regardless of how long they've been here.

My escort stops outside of an ornate set of double doors and reaches into her apron pocket. My heart rate picks up until she pulls out my knife, the one Trainwreck gave me.

"Our Lord asked me to return this to you. It was found in Mr. Brick's bag."

"Why does he want me to have it back? Isn't he afraid I'll use it on him?"

"Our Lord has no fears."

Miss Doe turns the knobs on the doors and pushes them open. With a hand on my upper back, she urges me inside the library. Brick is sitting in a chair, his face pinched, angry. And standing in front of a grand fireplace is who I can only assume is Lord Luxuria. He's wearing a long black robe with a hood pulled up over his head.

"You're not gonna believe this, Syl." Brick laughs but there's a lack of humor in it. Hatred, yes. Disgust, absolutely. Humor, not a hint.

"I'm having a hard time believing a lot of things lately, Brick. You'll have to be more specific."

Lord Luxuria picks that moment to turn around and lower the hood.

"He's referring to me."

My jaw drops. This is something we didn't have right at all. Lord Luxuria, leader of a cult that survives on the sale of others, gets off on the pain and degradation of anyone they can get their hands on, is a woman.

I. Did. Not. See. That. Coming.

"Please, Sylvia, have a seat."

Shock continues to plague me, and I do as I'm told without thinking.

"Told ya," Brick says.

Lord Luxuria—or would it be Lady?—lunges forward and slaps Brick across the face. I wait for him to react, in any way, but he doesn't. He sits there and takes it like a little bitch.

"There will be no more of that," she hisses. "I may have let you into my home because you had something I wanted but don't mistake my hospitality for weakness or for forgiveness for your transgressions."

"What transgressions?" Brick counters.

"I've lost a client and another soldier because of you. Not to mention the money she would have brought in." She tilts her head in my direction.

"None of that is my fault. I didn't expect another MC to get involved."

"Are you kidding me?" I snort. "My sister and brother-in-law are part of that *other MC*. Of course they'd get involved."

"She's right." Lord Luxuria scowls at Brick. "You should always calculate every possible outcome before acting. You failed to do that and there will be consequences for that failure."

Brick says nothing. What can he say? She's not pointing out anything but the obvious.

"I hate to stop this... berating of Brick, but who the hell are you?" I ask. "I know you call yourself Lord Luxuria, but it can't come as a surprise that I was expecting a man."

"Does my name matter? Will it change anything for you?"

"No." I refrain from lying to this woman. It's a chance I'm not willing to take. I have no clue what she already knows about me, what secrets Brick has divulged. "I'm curious is all."

She chuckles and the sound runs through me like fingernails on a chalkboard. It's high pitched, scratchy, and just a tad creepy.

"Since you asked so nicely. My name is Mrs. Templeton. Conrad Templeton was my husband."

Conrad Templeton? Conrad Templeton?

I snap my fingers. "He was the founder and original Lord Luxuria, right?"

"That's correct."

"Why let people think you're a man?"

Even though she's the reason for so many people's pain and anguish, I still support equal rights. I'm not the monster in this story, after all.

"Many of our members don't know Mr. Templeton is dead. I'd prefer to keep it that way. Besides, people respect men, bow to them even. I have no interest in tearing apart what my husband created and if they knew I was running things, that would be exactly what happens."

Damn, the longer I sit here and listen to her, the more I find myself respecting her.

"Now, you're out of questions." She glances at the grandfather clock in the corner. "And based on my calculations, we're almost out of time." Mrs. Templeton claps her hands together and mood shifts to an almost giddy state. "So, now I'll give you what you want."

"You're going to let me go?"

"Not a chance," she quips. "But when your Tyler shows up, I'll be sure to kill you first, so you don't have to watch him die."

So much for respect.

"You listened to my call?" I know the answer, but I have no interest in getting Miss Doe in trouble.

"Of course. But you knew that, didn't you?"

"How would I know that?"

Mrs. Templeton's entire demeanor shifts in a flash. She lunges at me, and I'm so startled by the sudden change, I forget I have my knife. Hell, I've forgotten this entire time because I've been so entranced by what she has to say.

Stupid, stupid, stupid.

Delicate hands wrap around my throat, cutting off my air supply. I wheeze as I try to suck in a breath and after a few seconds, she lets me go and shoves me backward to the point my chair almost topples over.

"Do you really think I'm unaware of the blind spots throughout my own home? Please, they're there for a reason. I have to know I can trust my own staff, now don't I?"

"I'm not following."

"Each uniform has a tiny mic sewed into it. I hear everything that goes on, every *warning* they might give. The moment Miss Doe stopped you in that hallway, she was as good as dead."

"But she stopped me from escaping," I protest. "That has to count for something."

"One good deed doesn't cancel out a previous transgression. If it did..." She turns toward Brick. "... he would get to walk out of here today. With quite a bit of money actually."

"What good deed has he done?"

"He brought you to me, didn't he? And kept me apprised of your little group's location from the moment you left Oregon. You didn't think that the attack on the van was a coincidence, did you?"

I glare at Brick. "No, I just didn't know he was responsible."

"He wasn't responsible," she snaps. "I was! He just made it possible."

"Okay."

The clock chimes, and Mrs. Templeton grins.

"Oh, things are about to get fun. They're almost here."

I can only assume she means the Soulless Kings and Black Savages. How the hell does she know what time they'll be here? I don't even know, other than after dark.

In this moment, regret washes through me at having contacted Trainwreck. Because of my overconfidence, she knows they're coming. She might not know the specifics of what's planned, but I'm not sure that matters. She's got eyes and ears everywhere and she'll figure it out. Mrs. Templeton is by no means a stupid woman.

Mrs. Templeton walks to a bookshelf and grabs a book, only to open it and take out a gun. While her back is turned, I whisper to Brick.

"Please tell me you have a weapon."

"Nope. She didn't give me mine back like she did yours. If only she knew what you're capable of."

"Dammit."

"What was that, Sylvia?" the woman asks, pointing the gun in my direction.

"Nothing. I just hiccupped."

She stares at me, and I wait for the consequence for my lie, but it doesn't come. She shifts the gun and points it at Brick.

"Stand up," she commands, and Brick does as he's told. "Walk to that shelf across the room." She points to another bookshelf that is identical to the one she's standing in front of.

As Brick starts to walk, there's a loud commotion in the hallway. The door bursts open and Trainwreck rushes in. At the same time, the bookshelf Brick is walking toward crashes to the floor and Squirrel climbs over them, firing at Lord Luxuria as he does. Three shots to the chest and she collapses, dead.

Before I can process how Squirrel even got past the bookshelf, Brick lunges for my knife, but instead of taking it from me, he brings it up to my neck and turns me toward Trainwreck.

Chapter Twenty-Six

My last thought before hitting the pavement is that what I'm seeing is probably just a figment of my dying imagination.

Trainwreck

Sweat trickles down my back as I train my gun on Brick. With Sylvia in front of him, I can't get a clean shot. I look at Squirrel, who's behind Brick and shake my head. *Don't shoot.* I can't risk his bullet going through Brick and hitting her.

"We both know you're not going to kill me."

I smirk at Brick. "Really? I don't know any such thing."

"How did you get the drop on her?" Brick asks. "She's got eyes everywhere."

"And we've got the best hacker in the country." Brick narrows his eyes, so I explain it to him. "You're forgetting I've dedicated the last few years to studying this cult. I know everything that was out there about them." I glance down at Lord Luxuria. "Well, I didn't know she was a woman. Kudos to her for *that* secret." I raise my head up.

"Anyway, once the club got involved, that meant I had access to Squirrel's expertise. He figured out the security system pretty quickly and between hacking that and the blueprints..." I shrug. "We figured shit out. And discovered the hidden doorways in the rooms on the first floor that led to..." I nod toward the bookcase that Squirrel came over. "Ta-da. You guessed it, the library."

"None of that was given as part of the plan," Brick snarls and holds the blade closer to Sylvia's throat. "How is anyone supposed to carry out a plan when they don't know all the details?"

"C'mon, Brick," I taunt. "You're not that stupid."

Static comes through on my two-way radio and I grab it out of my cut. I depress the button so I can talk into it.

"Yeah?"

"All secured on our end," Greaser says, though the words come through choppy.

"They're all out?"

"Those that were still alive. It looks like Lord Luxuria had his men kill as many as possible before we arrived."

"Her men."

"What?"

"Lord Luxuria... should be Lady Luxuria. The new leader was a woman. Squirrel took her out."

"Damn." Greaser whistles. "Do you have Sylvia?"

"Affirmative. But we're dealing with an issue. Get the explosives set up and ready and wait fifteen minutes. If we're not out by then, blow the place up."

"No, T. Not gonna happen."

"Greaser, I'm in charge here, remember? Do as you're told."

"The plan was to wait until we saw you clear the circular driveway in front of the mansion."

"Plans change."

"I don't like this, T. What about Sylvia? And what am I supposed to tell Fender and Charlie."

"You don't have to like it. You just have to follow orders. As for Sylvia, we've talked about what would happen if the plan went south. We're good on our end."

There's a moment of silence and then a muffled, "Fine."

"And Greaser, if things go south…"

"I'll take care of Trinity."

"Tell her I love her."

"You got it."

The walkie goes silent, and I shove it back into my cut.

"She killed them all?" Sylvia asks, a sheen glossing her eyes.

"Not all. Some. But don't focus on that, Syl. Focus on me, okay?"

"You should focus on the blade pressing against your throat, babe," Brick snarls. "Trainwreck can't help you now." He tosses a look over his shoulder. "Or the tech nerd."

"Ignore him, Sylvia. He's just trying to get into your head."

"I wouldn't be so sure about that. If I'm not mistaken, neither of you have a shot. My weapon, on the other hand, is exactly where it needs to be to inflict the most damage." Brick's tone is cavalier, matter of fact. "I slice Sylvia up, you'll be so broken hearted I'll be able to take you out easily. And then him… he'll be upset by your death and poof, he's gone." Brick shifts so his back is to neither Squirrel nor me. "Or, better yet, I slice her up and let you live. Imagine that, the rest of your life without her. Yeah, I think that's the better option."

I can't imagine it. I don't want to. A life without Sylvia would be torture. We may have only been giving this thing between us a chance, but I'm done with chances. What Greaser said about love may have confused me in the moment, but right here, right now, it's crystal fucking clear. I do love her. Because the thought of losing her today, or any day for that matter, is unfathomable.

"If you kill her, I kill you," I sneer. "You don't want to die, do ya Brick?"

"At least I'll go out knowing I caused your devastation, your downfall. I'll go out knowing you can't have her anymore." Brick smirks. "I'll die a happy man."

He's fucking crazy. He's so focused on my misery that he's bound to screw up. And maybe, just maybe, there's still a way to get Sylvia out of here.

"Squirrel, get gone."

"Not leaving you, Trainwreck."

"Yes, you are."

"I'll go when you and Sylvia go."

"That's not how this is going to work, Squirrel. Please, I need you to go."

Squirrel lowers his gun and turns toward me. "Trainwreck, are you sure? I knew exactly what I signed on for when I volunteered to come in here with you. I'm not afraid to die."

"Go."

Squirrel looks back toward Brick and Sylvia before walking out the door. Good. Now I can focus on getting myself and my woman out. I don't need to worry about anyone else but the two of us.

Sylvia looks up at the clock. Seven minutes have passed since I talked to Greaser. She's as aware of what's at stake as I am.

"Tyler, what's the plan?"

"Yeah, *Tyler*, what's the plan?" Brick mimics.

"Give me a minute."

"I'll give you five," Sylvia states, her tone calm, full of trust. "But after that, we need to be running."

"You two disgust me. I can't believe you chose him over me, babe. That was a big mistake." Brick puts more pressure on the knife, and Sylvia winces when it knicks her. Blood beads under the blade. "If you're so set on getting blown to bits, fine. But I'm getting the fuck out of here."

The next ten seconds seem to happen in slow motion, and it feels as if I'm outside of my body, watching it all take place.

Brick shoves Sylvia to the floor, where she skids toward the Lady's pistol, and then he throws Sylvia's Stabbing Grace at me. I pull the trigger on the gun I'm holding but only manage to graze Brick's shoulder as the knife pierces my side.

Sylvia picks up the pistol and rolls to her back, squeezing the trigger and unloading all the rounds into Brick. When he falls to the floor, she crawls toward me and takes my gun. Sylvia stands and slowly walks toward Brick. He tries to scoot away from her, but she kicks him in the nuts. Brick howls in pain but the sound doesn't last long.

"This is for what you put me through," Sylvia sneers right before she pulls the trigger and puts a hole in Brick's head.

Her shoulders slump, relief hitting her hard.

"Syl," I call to her. Searing pain travels through my body and my teeth begin to chatter. "You need to get out of here."

Sylvia scrambles toward me and drops to her knees. "I'm not leaving you." She shoves an arm under me and helps me sit up. "You can walk, Tyler. With my help, you can walk." She rises to her feet and tries to haul me to mine. "C'mon, you need to try."

"I..." My head is spinning. "I can't."

"Yes, you can," she insists. "Don't make me drag you."

"You sh-should know," I push out. "I l-love you."

"I love you too, now c'mon on! We can talk about our feelings later."

I try to help Sylvia as much as I can. I manage to get to my feet and take a few steps before falling to my knees.

"Good, Tyler. Now we just need to do that, oh, a hundred more times."

I fight the dizziness, the nausea, for as long as I can. I use every ounce of strength the stab wound hasn't already taken, and we get to the front door. As Sylvia pulls it open, I see the outline of my brothers at the edge of the property. Or at least I think I do.

My knees buckle, and my last thought before hitting the pavement is that what I'm seeing is probably just a figment of my dying imagination.

Chapter Twenty-Seven

I think we can make that happen.

Sylvia

"That's the last one."

I twist in the front seat of the panel van Fender stole so I can see into the back. Trainwreck is sprawled out on the blankets one of the brothers had in his saddle bags. Gibson, the Soulless Kings' doc, is sitting next to him, his hands covered in blood, his face drawn and tired.

"He'll be okay?" I ask Gibson.

"He should be. The stab wound didn't hit any vital organs, that I can tell. The stitches should do the trick, as long as he doesn't do anything to pop them out."

"When do you think he'll wake up?" Greaser asks from the driver's seat. He glances at Gibson in the rearview mirror for a second but otherwise remains focused on the road.

"I gave him a mild sedative to help him sleep through

what I had to do. Since he regained consciousness before I did that, and he's not still out from an injury to the head, I'd say he should wake up before we stop for the night."

"Did you call Trinity?" I ask Greaser. After getting Trainwreck to the door, everything happened so fast, and I've been so wrapped up in my own mind that I forgot about his twin sister.

"Yeah. I'll call her again when we stop, give her an update."

"Okay, good." I nod. "That's good."

"Sylvia, why don't you try to get some rest?" Gibson rests a hand on my shoulder.

"Trainwreck is going to be fine and there's nothing you can do while we're on the road."

"I'm fine."

"Sylvia." Greaser's tone holds a warning.

I turn to face forward and let my head fall back against the headrest. "Not you too," I whine, not giving a damn how childish I sound. I'm too tired to care.

"Yes, me too. You're one of us now. T has claimed you which means you're forever tied to the rest of the Soulless Kings."

"What about the Black Savages?"

I know how Charlie handled things but I'm not sure how I should. Do I even have a choice?

"That's up to you. You grew up with them, and it would make sense if you didn't want to cut ties. It would also make sense if you did, considering everything that went down. No one is gonna tell you what the right choice is. Only you know that."

I let my mind process Greaser's words of wisdom and drift off to sleep. I don't know how much time passes, but when I wake up, we're in the parking lot of yet another hotel. I'm so sick of hotels. Wishing I wasn't relegated to one, I climb out of the van and walk to the back to help Trainwreck get out.

"Hey sleepyhead," he teases when I come into his view. "You've been out for a while."

I throw my arms around his neck, almost knocking him over onto his back. Trainwreck groans in pain and guilt slams into me. I try to pull away, but he holds me tight.

"I'm so sorry," I whisper. "So fucking sorry."

"For what? Hugging me?"

"Hurting you."

"Sylvia, I'm fine. I'd rather feel a little pain because of a hug than no pain and have you away from me."

I nod into his shoulder.

"Did you mean it, Syl? What you said back there?"

"I said a lot of things."

"You know what I'm talking about."

"Did you mean it when you said it?"

"It took me some time to figure out that the emotions and feelings were there, but once I did? Fuck, the world brightened up. So, yeah, I meant it. I love you."

"I love you too."

Trainwreck presses his lips to mine. The kiss isn't fevered like every other time we've kissed. It's gentle, sweet... nice, like the man delivering it. And right now, I am all for a whole lotta nice.

"Okay, you two, time to get a room."

Both Trainwreck and I laugh at Greaser. Surprisingly, I don't think he actually cares if we get a room so he doesn't have to watch us make out. I think he's more concerned with actual sleep.

"When we take off tomorrow, we're driving straight through, so we all need to get as much sleep as we can tonight. Some of the others are already here and the rest will join us when their done."

The hair on the back of my neck stands on end. "Done doing what?"

"Whatever boss man here instructed them to do." Greaser nods at Trainwreck.

"You're not gonna tell me, are you?" I ask.

"It doesn't matter," Trainwreck assures me. "You did your part, let them do theirs."

"Fine. But if we're going to be together, we're gonna have to figure something out. I don't like being kept in the dark."

"Syl, you know what it's like. There are only so many rules I can bend. Sharing club business with my ol' lady isn't one of them."

"I'm not your ol' lady."

"Girlfriend, then. Stop quibbling over semantics. You know exactly what I meant."

I heave a sigh. "If you have your rules, then I have mine."

"Okay, what are they?"

"No restrictions on knives."

"Done. What else?"

I stand there and realize that's all I've got. "That's it."

"Great. But just one thing."

"What?"

"Next time I buy you a knife, can we try to make sure *I'm* not stabbed with it?"

I throw my head back and laugh. "I think we can make that happen."

Trainwreck

The pounding on our hotel room door pulls me from a deep sleep. A quick glance at Trainwreck assures me he's still asleep, so I get out of bed and trudge toward the door. I look through the peephole and see Donovan standing there, covered in what appears to be ash and dirt.

I slide the chain over and yank open the door.

"What happened to you?" I demand, concern flaring through me.

Donovan looks to his left and then his right. "Can I come in?"

I look over my shoulder at Trainwreck and see he's still sleeping. Rather than invite Donovan in, I step out into the hall and hold the door open with my foot so I can get back in.

"What is going on? Why are you so dirty?"

"A bunch of us stayed behind to make sure there was nothing left that could trace back to either club. We also gave statements to law enforcement."

"Why would you do that? What if—"

"This isn't anyone's first rodeo, Syl. We knew what we were doing." Donovan smiles. "We told them we were out on a club ride, passed the compound and saw the flames, and then called nine-one-one. Nothing is going to come back on us. We're good."

"If the house was still on fire, how were you able to be sure there was nothing left behind?"

"Trainwreck and Squirrel pulled some strings, made sure we had the right equipment to get in."

"Well isn't he just full of secrets?" I mutter.

"That's the other thing I wanted to talk to you about."

"Look, Donovan, I may not like the secrets, but I understand them. So, if you're gonna give me a speech about how he's not right for me, save it."

"All I wanted to say was I think he's a keeper." My eyebrows shoot up and he continues. "I know I haven't been his biggest fan, but he did good tonight. Hell, he's done good through this whole thing. Besides, I've realized, it's not my place to tell you who you can and can't date. I don't know that my judgment is right anyway."

I rest a hand on Donovan's arm. "Brick wasn't your fault. You know that, right?"

"I know. Doesn't make it an easier pill to swallow."

A noise comes from the hotel room, and I quickly peek in at Trainwreck. He's stirring but I don't think he's awake.

"I better let you get back in there." Donovan turns to walk away but stops to look back at me. "We've always got room for you, and so does your mom, but something tells me you won't need it."

"Are you giving me your blessing, Donovan?"

"Not that you need it." He winks at me. "But yeah, I am."

Epilogue

I need her... naked... writhing beneath me.

Trainwreck
Six months later...

"I'd like to make a toast."

Someone lowers the volume of the music down, and all eyes turn toward Fender. He raises his shot glass, and everyone in the clubhouse does the same with their drinks.

"To taking down the Church of Sinfinite Opportunity!" A chorus of cheers follows. "And to nothing leading back to the Soulless Kings or the Black Savages as the investigation is closed!"

When we got back from Arkansas, Fender made contact with the club's attorney, Alan Forney. He explained the situation so Alan could keep an eye on the investigation. We got the phone call today that the case is closed, and the fire was ruled a murder/suicide. The suspect? Lady Luxuria.

There has been endless news coverage about the

Church and its followers. So much so, that anyone who still remained is afraid to operate any more for fear of being caught. We really did it. We really took them down.

I climb up on the table next to Fender. "I'd like to add to that." I raise my glass. "To all of you for believing in me and trusting that I could lead that mission!"

"Here, here!"

Fender and I jump off the table, and he signals to Margo for another round.

"You did good, T." He taps his glass to mine and then nods toward Sylvia, who's standing across the room with her sister. "Did good there, too."

Greaser comes up behind us and wraps his arms around our shoulders. "So, when are you popping the question?"

"Don't know."

"Aw, c'mon, bro," Greaser pleads. "I wanna know when we're all gonna be legal brothers and shit."

"Fuck me," Fender groans. "I don't need to be legally bound to either of you clowns."

"You know you love us, Prez," I tease.

"Yeah, I do. But I don't need to be jabbering about it at a club party." He shakes Greaser off of him and walks away, grumbling about 'feelings and shit'.

"He's so easy to get worked up."

"Why did you have to bring me into it?"

"Because, T. You're my brother-in-law and soon, you'll be his. It's time you learn how brothers work."

"I know how brothers work, dude. I've been part of the club for years now."

"Not those kind of brothers."

Greaser saunters away and joins Trinity at the bar. Margo brings me the rounds Fender signaled for and of course, she feels the need to add her two cents.

"For what it's worth, I think you should go for it. Sylvia's a great girl."

Why is everyone choosing tonight to tell me how to live my life? I've got enough on my mind without their input. I shake their voices out of my head and cross the room to Sylvia.

"Hey you," she says and wraps her arms around me. "I was wondering when I'd get your attention tonight."

"You always have my attention, Syl, and you know it."

"True. You are kind of obsessed with me."

I pull her close and bury my face in the crook of her neck. "I'm obsessed with this body of yours, that's for sure."

She reaches between us and shoves her hand down my pants to grip my cock. A growl barrels out of my throat at her touch.

"And I'm obsessed with this." She squeezes me. "Why don't we take this party back to our place?"

Our place. I'll never get tired of hearing that. Sylvia moved in with me as soon as we got back from Arkansas. Neither of us are the type to drag things out and we both knew at that point what we wanted: each other.

"Not yet. I've got one more thing to do before we can leave."

"Make it quick."

I remove her hand from my jeans and press a kiss to her palm. "I'll try."

I walk back to the middle of the room and get back on the table Fender and I occupied not ten minutes ago.

"Yo, everyone, shut up for a minute!" I shout.

Again, the music is lowered.

"What more could you possibly say, Trainwreck?" someone yells.

"Yeah, I'd rather hear the music than you babbling."

I listen to all the taunts and laugh at most of them. They don't bother me. There was a time in my life I would have taken them personally but not anymore. I recognize them for what they are: signs of brotherhood.

"I won't be long." I turn toward Sylvia. "Syl, can you come up here?" Sylvia looks at me suspiciously and hesitates. "I won't bite. That comes later."

She throws her head back and laughs and then comes to join me on the table.

"What are you doing?" she asks in a harsh whisper.

"Yeah, T, what are you doing?" Greaser shouts from across the room.

"I said I'd make this quick so here goes." I get down on one knee and grab the box from my pocket. I lift the lid and grin. "Sylvia, will you marry me?"

Her hands fly to her mouth, and tears well in her eyes. Sylvia isn't an overly emotional person. A ball buster, a bad ass, but not emotional. Those tears are how I know I've managed to surprise her when her guard was down.

"I thought you said you didn't know when you were going to do this?"

"He's good at keeping secrets, Greaser," Sylvia calls over her shoulder around a wet laugh, but her eyes never leave mine. "Tyler, are you serious?"

"Do I look serious?" She nods. "Then yeah, Syl, I'm dead serious. Will you marry me?"

"Yes, of course I'll marry you." She falls to her knees and throws her arms around my neck. "I love you so much."

"I love you too."

"Now can we go upstairs. We've got a lot to celebrate." She leans close to whisper in my ear, "Alone."

I slide the ring onto her finger and help her off the table.

As I guide her across the room, we're congratulated, over and over again. We stop and talk to a few of the brothers and to her sister, but I don't let the conversations go on too long.

I need her... naked... writhing beneath me.

The side door to the clubhouse flies open with a bang.

"Get down on the ground. Now!"

Sylvia and I exchange a look before dropping to our stomachs. I keep an arm around her but lift my head to see who came charging in.

The white lettering on the black uniforms turn my blood cold. SWAT.

"We're looking for Travis 'Squirrel' Kramer. Where is he?"

Squirrel? What is this about? Was our attorney wrong and the investigation not closed?

My mind spins with possibilities.

"What is this about?"

I catch sight of Fender's boots as he walks toward the SWAT team.

"Sir, get down on the ground."

"With all due respect, I know my rights. I'm unarmed, my hands are in the air where you can see them, and I'm only asking a question. What do you want with Squirrel?"

"We'll discuss that with him, sir."

"Fender, it's okay." Squirrel's voice booms from across the room. He addresses the SWAT team next. "I'm Travis. Also unarmed."

"Get on your knees," an officer commands. "Now."

I lift my head and twist to my side so I can see what's happening. Squirrel drops to his knees and puts his hands on the back of his head. He's been through this before, so he knows the drill.

Another SWAT team member rushes forward and yanks Squirrel's hands behind his back.

"Travis 'Squirrel' Kramer, you're under arrest for the murder of Maria Sampson. You have the right to remain silent..."

The rest of his rights trail off as I focus on the name. Maria Sampson, Maria Sampson, Maria Sampson. Who the fuck is she?

"Squirrel, you say nothing until Alan gets there, you hear me?" Fender calls out to him as he's dragged out of the clubhouse. "Not a word."

A man dressed in a black suit comes inside just as Squirrel is taken away. "You can have his attorney meet him here. That's where he's being taken."

I watch Fender take the card, but he doesn't look at it until every law enforcement agent is gone. I rush to his side and look over his shoulder.

"Prez, that card says he's being taken to Michigan. When the hell was he in Michigan?"

Fender pulls out his cell phone and taps on Alan Forney's phone number in his contacts list. While he waits for him to answer, he responds to me.

"As far as I know, never."

Next in the Soulless Kings MC Series

Squirrel...

Don't talk. Never give up your brothers if you get caught. If you go down, you go down... *alone.* That's just one of the things drilled into us as Soulless Kings. There are other rules, of course, but sitting in a jail cell, that is the only one running through my head. What's worse, I'm sitting here for a crime I didn't commit.

Normally, I wouldn't worry because the club has a damn good attorney on retainer, but he's not the one who walks through the door for my first attorney-client meeting. No, it's a public defender who looks fresh out of college with a degree in sexy nerd. All she's missing is a pocket protector and suspenders. I might as well plead guilty on the first-degree murder charge and resign myself to life in prison.

And then she opens that pretty little mouth of hers and hope flares.

Lexi...

My parents were so proud of me when I graduated from Harvard Law. When I told them I wanted to be a public defender instead of some high-powered prosecutor, that pride disappeared, because that wasn't their plan for me. To them, being a public defender wasn't going to get my family out of the Bronx. It wasn't going to elevate their lives the way they thought they deserved after all their sacrifices. But I didn't care.

My caseload has been challenging, but rewarding. I've helped a lot of innocent people and sure, I've probably helped a few not-so-innocent assholes walk. But that's the job, and I love it... until now. Sitting across from the scary biker who rightfully deserves to go down for murder, I'm scared for the first time in two years.

And then he opens his mouth, and I question everything I thought I knew before walking into this meeting.

Also by Andi Rhodes

Broken Rebel Brotherhood

Broken Souls

Broken Innocence

Broken Boundaries

Broken Rebel Brotherhood: Complete Series Box set

Broken Rebel Brotherhood: Next Generation

Broken Hearts

Broken Wings

Broken Mind

Bastards and Badges

Stark Revenge

Slade's Fall

Jett's Guard

Soulless Kings MC

Fender

Joker

Piston

Greaser

Riker

Trainwreck

Squirrel

Gibson

Satan's Legacy MC

Snow's Angel

Toga's Demons

Magic's Torment

About the Author

Andi Rhodes is an author whose passion is creating romance from chaos in all her books! She writes MC (motorcycle club) romance with a generous helping of suspense and doesn't shy away from the more difficult topics. Her books can be triggering for some so consider yourself warned. Andi also ensures each book ends with the couple getting their HEA! Most importantly, Andi is living her real life HEA with her husband and their boxers.

For access to release info, updates, and exclusive content, be sure to sign up for Andi's newsletter at andirhodes.com.

Printed in Great Britain
by Amazon